SUNSETS AT PELICAN BEACH

PELICAN BEACH SERIES BOOK TWO

MICHELE GILCREST

CONTENTS

LEXI

$\mathcal{C}$ole and his crew carefully carried in the granite for my parents' new center island. Once it was in place, he stood back, admiring the cut and gliding his hand along the surface. She chose the most elegant European granite that Cole could find. It was just like her to spare no expense. Dad gave his stamp of approval but really didn't care about the details. I stood nearby in the dining area, admiring his skills and other aspects of him as I prepared lunch. In a little while, I'd head back to the boutique, but not before seeing to it that Cole had everything he needed.

"Lexi, that's quite a spread you have there," he said.

As a client and long time friend of Cole's family, I thought it was only right to take good care.

"Yes, I made it for you and the crew. I thought you might need a little fuel to help you get through the rest of the day."

"I know the guys will appreciate it. You really didn't have to do this. I'm sure you're already busy with running the boutique. Coming over here during the day and feeding us is way beyond your call of duty."

"It's no big deal. I promised I would be here to help Mom oversee things whenever she couldn't be here."

Cole whistled for the crew members working outside to get their attention.

"Everybody, Miss Donovan has some food here for you. I'll take care of the counter while you guys go ahead and take a lunch break."

He turned back toward me.

"You're going to have some, too, aren't you? There's a variety to choose from. Over here, you have turkey or ham and cheese on croissants, and then you also have..."

"Thank you, Lexi. I appreciate it. I really do. However, my girlfriend, Payton, should be stopping by any moment now. Usually, once a week, she whips together a surprise lunch for me. I'd hate to disappoint her by spoiling my appetite."

"Oh, I see. That's awfully nice of her. Does she make it a habit to come to your worksite?"

"She doesn't stay long. My clients don't normally have an issue with it, but if it's a problem, I can call her."

"Oh, no. Don't be silly. I wouldn't give it another thought. I'll just lay the tray of food over here, so it doesn't interfere with your workspace."

I laid the tray on a table that was out of the way. I was irritated at the idea of Payton stopping by. I didn't want his time at the house to end without me telling Cole that I was in love with him. With a little encouragement, hopefully, he'd realize that I was perfect for him. We were perfect for each other.

"Cole, I have to get ready to head back to the boutique. My mother and I are swapping this afternoon. I'm covering the boutique while she'll be here with the crew. Before I go, I was wondering if you heard about the fundraiser that we're hosting for the young boys and girls club?"

"No, I wasn't aware."

"It's going to be a huge event. All of the proceeds will go to the children. We thought it would be a great way to give back to the community. Hopefully, if we can get all the locals with deep pockets to participate, we can raise enough funds to provide school supplies, activities, and new clothing to the children this year."

"Well, that certainly sounds like a good cause. I'm all for anything that will benefit the kids."

"I figured you would be. I was thinking this might be a good opportunity for you and your daughter, Emmie, to get involved. I know how much she loves to help out."

"Really? What did you have in mind?"

"Mom wants to have a live auction at the fundraiser. She's been in touch with quite a few business owners to ask them to donate some of their services."

Cole leaned back on the counter and folded his arms.

"That makes sense for businesses like the bakery that could offer a free gift basket, or the nail salon that could offer a... what do you ladies call it?"

"A mani-pedi?" I said.

"Yes, a mani-pedi or a spa day. But I'm not sure my business falls in line with all of the other services."

"Yes, but there is something else you could offer."

"And what's that?"

"Perhaps a small donation and spreading the word around Pelican Beach, of course. But even more importantly, we want you to be there with sweet Emmie."

"Oh, Lexi, I'm happy to give a donation, but I don't know about..."

"Now, now. Think about how helpful it would be for you to attend and mingle with the town officials. Come on. You know them all on a first-name basis because they all speak highly of your renovation work. Your reputation spreads beyond Pelican Beach and is well known here in Naples as well."

"Yes, but.."

"And... perhaps if you're there, you can encourage the donors to give up a little bit more money for the fundraiser. Emmie can help out with the games, and you can feel good in knowing you did it for a great cause. It's a win-win for all!"

He stood scratching his rugged beard. I knew I was starting to warm him up to the idea by his slowly emerging smile. I think deep down, Cole always did have an interest in me. All I needed was a little more time, and Payton Matthews would be a thing of the past.

"Lexi, you sure do drive a hard bargain."

"Yes, but a hard bargain for a very good cause. Wouldn't you agree?"

"Yesss, you can sign me up. But only under one condition."

"Anything, you name it."

I stood in front of him, trying to look as irresistible as possible.

"No tricks on the day of the fundraiser, Lexi. I mean it. You're not putting me in a dunking tank, I'm not going on any dates, and I'm not doing anything crazy. I'm just there to show support."

"You got it. Note to self. No dunking tanks and no dates, for now."

"Lexiiiii."

"Just kidding." I adjusted the collar on his shirt, which was a little out of place.

"In the meantime, be sure to ask Emmie to think about if she'd prefer to help with games or the cotton candy booth."

"Ha, that's a no brainer, but I'll let her know."

His daughter Emmie was the cutest little thing. She always looked so darling in the dresses that we sent her from the boutique. I'm confident it wouldn't be hard to win her affection as a stepmother. My family has known Emmie and Cole's mother for years. Yet another advantage to add to the list if you ask me.

Just then, the doorbell rang.

"That's probably Payton," he said.

It was all I could do not to grit my teeth. I mean, could the man work in peace without having her checking on him? Or maybe she was here to check on me? Either way, if she wanted to come by and see what was going on, I'd be happy to give her a little show.

"I'll get the door." I offered.

I noticed him catching a glimpse of me as I walked out of the kitchen. It was probably my new dress that hugged my silhouette just so. Through the stained glass, I could see Miss Perfect standing with a bag in one hand and a cooler in another. I opened the door.

"Payton, darling. How are you?"

She gave me a fake smile and seemed rather shocked.

"Hi, Lexi. I'm pretty good. How are you doing?"

"Oh, I can't complain. And if I did, no one would listen anyway. It's been a while. I don't think I've seen you since our last photo shoot."

I let her continue to stand just outside of the door, hoping that she would get the message that I didn't want her to come in.

"Let me guess. Is all of this for Cole?"

"Yes, it is. I normally surprise him with lunch when my schedule allows."

She proceeded to step inside the house, but I shifted so she couldn't get past me.

"Lunch. Yes, that's right. He mentioned that you'd be stopping by. Unfortunately, the kitchen is literally in shambles right now. Cole asked me to thank you and to collect the lunch, so you didn't have to get in harm's way."

Those weren't his exact words, but there was no harm in keeping her out of a kitchen that was under construction.

"Well, I normally say a quick hello. It won't take but a minute," Payton said.

"It's fine. You can hand everything over to me. I'll be sure he gets it. Mom would have a nervous breakdown if she thought someone was in her kitchen and could potentially get hurt."

She finally handed over the bag and the cooler.

"Do me a favor, Lexi. Please tell Cole that I packed all of his favorites and ask him to give me a call when he has a chance."

"Certainly. Don't worry; I'll get right on it."

Behind her, I could see the palm trees starting to sway and some dark clouds rolling in.

"Oh, Payton, it looks like a storm is heading in. You should be on your way. Be safe, dear."

Since my hands were full, I closed the door with my foot and returned to the kitchen.

"Lunch is here."

"Awesome, where's Payton?" Cole was looking beyond where I was standing.

"There's an awful storm kicking up, so she had to run. She did ask me to give you this contraption of a cooler, and this bag."

"Thanks. I'm surprised she didn't want to come in. Even if it was only to say a quick hello, she didn't say anything else?"

"No. I'm sure she was concerned about heading back before the storm lets loose."

"Hmm."

"Well, you go ahead and eat. I'm going to check on my mother and let her know she may want to delay heading back until the storm passes."

He bit into his apple while glancing out the kitchen window.

"Yeah, I guess I didn't do a good enough job at checking the forecast."

I really had my work cut out for me if I was going to win Cole over. It seemed completely unfair that Payton would just show up in the last year and serve as a distraction. After his wife's passing, I provided an ear to listen and a shoulder when he needed it most. That's okay. She may be a little setback to my plans, but my mother didn't raise a little weakling.

PAYTON

$\mathcal{J}$t wasn't like Cole to not say hello when I stopped by to bring him lunch. And it certainly wasn't like him not to call me. I'd have to deal with all that later on. For now, I had one week until the grand opening of my photography store, and I was feeling pretty anxious. My dream was finally coming to fruition, and all I could do was worry. What if no one showed up for the grand opening? What if my shipment for the front display didn't arrive on time? I had so many thoughts swimming around in my head. Thankfully, Abby my sister, was here to help keep me sane.

"Would you like me to hang your new welcome sign on the front door?" Abby held the sign up, admiring the handcrafted beauty.

"Yes, that would be perfect. Thanks, Ab."

"Sure. I really think things are starting to come together. "

"Do you think?"

"Yes, Payton, you have to stop being so hard on yourself. Seriously, when I arrived today, I was expecting this place to be a mess, according to your description. But instead, it's just like the name of the store, 'Picture Perfect.' "

"Aww, thanks, Abby. It feels like I live here as of late, so I would hope it's starting to have the resemblance of a real business."

I managed to get a good deal on renting the store Cole discovered. Its location was not far from the center of town. I was surprised to see the place was still vacant. It turned out, the owner had taken the for rent sign down and was considering selling instead. We worked out a deal, and with a little help, this place was really starting to look nice.

"Payton, I'm going to give you a pass to work long hours now because you're just getting things up and running. After the opening, you have to promise me you're going to set decent hours for yourself."

I nodded but wasn't sure how realistic that would be.

"You do understand that I'm running this place by myself, right?"

"Understood. But, plans are in place to hire part-time help. You don't have to listen to me if you don't want to, but just recall the times we used to practically live at the Inn as little kids. Remember the long hours Mom and Dad used to work?"

"Yes, I can also recall it eventually paid off for them."

She walked over and rested her hands on my shoulders.

"Not before having an impact on Dad's health and forcing them into retirement."

"True."

Abby returned to breaking down boxes and popping bubble wrap.

"Besides, you have a love life to attend to and a potential step-daughter to spend time with."

I stared at the position of the coo-coo clock nestled in the corner.

"You're rather quiet over there. Is everything okay with you and Cole?"

"Everything is good, I guess."

"You guess? Alright, spill the beans. Something's bothering you. I know that sound when I hear it."

"It's nothing, really."

Abby gave me a blank stare. Probably because she knew I was a terrible liar.

"Everything is fine with Cole. It's Lexi that I'm concerned about."

"Lexi Donovan?"

"The one and only. She and her mother, who I affectionately refer to as Cruella, are on a mission to destroy our relationship."

I didn't know this to be a fact, but it sure did feel like it.

"I remember you saying something about them back when Mrs. Donovan was your client. That was a while ago. I thought surely everyone had moved on by now."

"Well, I guess I didn't mention it before now, but they persuaded Cole to do Mrs. Donovan's kitchen renovation."

"Persuaded? Come on, Payton. He is in the renovation business to make money. I'm sure all she had to do was call and book an appointment just like everyone else."

"Not so. Cole has been overbooked for months and kept telling her he wasn't sure he would be able to take on the job. He even went as far as offering some good recommendations of other companies that he works with on occasion. But nooo. Mrs. Donovan doesn't take no for an answer. I know first hand because it took forever for me to finally wrap up the photography job I had with her. That woman acted as if she was going to make me a permanent part of the staff."

"Okay," she said.

"They sent Emmie clothing from the boutique to kiss up to

Cole until he eventually caved in and said yes. Prior to him agreeing, she used to send Lexi over to his house to 'butter him up,' as she would say. And to make matters worse, Mrs. Donovan came right out and told me she thought Lexi was a good fit for Cole. As if she didn't already know we were dating."

"Now, that's a bit much!"

"Do you think?"

Abby put down the bubble wrap and rested her hand on her hips.

"Did you tell Cole?"

"Why? So I could risk looking like a jealous new girlfriend? Absolutely not! Besides, I didn't want to start giving Cole the impression that I didn't trust him. It's bad enough that I have trust issues from a failed marriage."

"Makes sense. But that was last year, Payton. If this is still going on, maybe you need to find a gentle way to bring it up."

"I'm two steps ahead of you! After what happened today, I'm definitely going to bring it up. I went over to their house to drop off his lunch just as I would normally do whenever I have the spare time. He's always welcomed the idea of me bringing lunch, and his clients never complain about it."

"Let me guess. Lexi was there?"

"Not only was she there, but she took the food, wouldn't let me in, and practically slammed the door in my face."

A slightly exaggerated version, but it's the principle that matters.

"Cole didn't come looking for you?"

"No. But only God knows what she may have told him."

"True," Abby said.

The telephone rang and startled the both of us. We laughed at the old push-button phone. It sounded like an alarm clock, but the vintage look fell right in line with my parlor theme.

I paused to clear my throat. "Picture Perfect."

"Payton, oh, I'm so glad I caught you."

"Mom? Are you okay?"

"Your father is missing. Please tell me either you or Abby have heard from him?"

"I haven't spoken to Dad since I left the house this morning. What's going on?"

"Is Abby with you?"

"Yes, she's been here with me for most of the day."

Abby was mouthing to me in the background, "What's wrong?"

I gave Abby a brief run down and asked her to check our cell phones. Maybe one of us had a missed call from Dad and didn't realize it.

"Mom, Abby's checking our phones. I know you're upset, but I need you to slow down for a minute and tell me what happened from start to finish."

Abby shook her head 'no' from across the room.

Mom took a deep breath and began to explain. "I left around ten this morning to run a few errands and go to the grocery store. I asked your father if he was coming with me, but he was tired and wanted to stay home. I had to go because we were out of some of our essentials. Long story short, I said I'd be back around noon and would prepare his lunch when I returned."

"What happened after that?"

"When I got back to the house, I noticed the door to our mailbox was wide open, so I walked over to close it. That's when I saw his house keys sitting on top of the mailbox. The keys were sitting there just as plain as day, and I thought to myself, maybe he came out here to get the mail and got distracted by something."

"That's odd."

Abby stood cheek to cheek, trying to hear what Mom was

saying. I guess the old phone was good for aesthetics but useless at the moment without the speaker option.

"I went into the house to look for your father and couldn't find him anywhere. The front door was locked. The bed was made. Everything is in order, but he's nowhere to be found."

Abby took over the phone.

"Mom, can you tell if Dad took his cell phone or his wallet with him?"

I stood, waiting to hear her response. It was unlike Dad to just take off without communicating with Mom.

"It's all right here on his nightstand."

"Okay, stay calm and try not to panic," Abby said.

I thought to pick up my cell phone and call our youngest sister, Rebecca. I knew she was at work, but perhaps she knew something that we didn't.

"Hello?" she answered.

"Becks, it's Payton. Have you heard from Dad this morning?"

"No. What's wrong?"

"Mom called us at the store. She can't seem to find Dad anywhere. The last time she saw him was before she left to run errands. When she got home, she found his keys on the mailbox, and there's no sign of Dad anywhere."

"What?"

"I know. It doesn't sound good, but I'm hoping there's some quirky explanation for it all. Maybe he's at the next-door neighbor's or somewhere close by and just forgot about his keys. Clearly, he intended to get the mail. Look, Abby and I are going to head over to the house. I'll call you with any updates."

"You don't have to. I'm leaving now."

"Okay, see you there."

Abby was already grabbing her bag when I got off the phone with Rebecca.

"Let's go, we can take my car," Abby said.

I grabbed my things, set the alarm, and locked everything up.

"Did Mom say anything else that might be helpful?" Abby continued to brainstorm.

"Not really. You can tell she's all out of sorts. I didn't want to press her much further. I figure when we get there, we can just split up and see if we can find him. Rebecca is meeting us at the house, so that's an extra pair of eyes."

"Or maybe she can stay with Mom to help keep her calm. Either way, I pray we can find him quickly."

"Abby?" My voice was a bit rattled.

"Payton, don't do it. Don't let your mind go there. Just think positive."

Everybody knew Dad was showing early signs of dementia. It seemed to be growing increasingly worse since my parents retired. But Abby was right. There was no point in letting my mind run wild with negative thoughts.

"I'm sure by the time we get there, Dad will be back in the house, safe and sound. He'll probably think we're the crazy ones for getting ourselves all worked up," she said.

"If he's not back, maybe we should circle around the neighborhood. I mean, how far could he really be on foot anyway?"

"Good point."

It didn't take long for us to make our way to our parents' house. As we pulled up, we could see Mom standing out front talking to the next-door neighbor. Abby put the car in park, and Rebecca pulled in behind us.

"Mom, any word from Dad yet?" I asked her.

She made her way across the front yard.

"No word. I'm so worried. I wonder if we should call the police. Your father has never pulled a stunt like this before."

"Try to stay calm, Mom." Rebecca tried to console her as best as she could.

"It's hard to stay calm. I just want to know where he is," she said.

"Okay, before we escalate things, why don't we split up and see if we can find him." Abby laid out a game plan that involved Rebecca staying by the house with Mom, while the two of us split up to search the surrounding area.

"Abby, do you have your cell phone on you?" I double-checked to be sure.

"Yes, fully charged. Call me right away if you find him."

Abby started heading down the street, so I figured I'd start with the beach. I was still living with my parents in their cottage, which was situated conveniently on Pelican Beach. There was only but so many places Dad could be in this small town. One of us had to find him.

I started calling out his name.

"Daaad. William Matthews, can you hear me?"

No response. There was nothing in sight except the entrance to the beach and the rear view of a few homes.

"Daaaad."

My phone buzzed in my hand. It was Cole.

"Hey, Cole."

"There you are. I missed you today. Did you make it back, alright?"

"I made it back fine."

"Lexi told me you were in a hurry because of the storm coming in."

"I wasn't exactly in a hurry, but I'm fine. We can talk about that later. Right now, I have an even bigger problem on my hands."

"What's the matter?"

"Abby and I are out searching for Dad. The last time my

15

Mom saw him was before she left to run errands. When she returned, he was nowhere to be found."

"You're kidding me."

"I wish I was. I'm on the beach now, but I don't see him. I'm going to head back and start looking around the neighborhood with Abby."

"Say no more. I'm packing up my things and heading over there now."

"Okay. Thanks, Cole."

"Payton?"

"Yes."

"We're going to find him. Everything will be fine."

"Thank you, Cole. That's exactly what I needed to hear."

"Okay, I'll be there soon. Love you."

"Love you too."

COLE

"*L*exi, I'm afraid I have to head out early today. I have an emergency that I have to tend to."

"Is everything alright?"

"Hopefully, it will be."

"Does it have to do with Emmie or your mother? I can go with you if you need help."

"Thank you, but they're fine. It's actually an emergency with Payton's family."

"Oh."

I gathered my tools while bringing Lexi up to speed.

"No need to worry. Please tell your mother that she's in good hands. The crew has everything they need. They'll continue working until the end of the day to keep everything on schedule, and I'll be back in the morning."

"It's awfully nice of you to drop everything at a moment's notice for the Matthews."

"Yeah, it's the least I can do. Payton means a lot to me."

I grabbed a few more items.

"That's interesting. I didn't think you two were serious. She doesn't seem like the type of woman you would choose for yourself or for Emmie."

"What makes you say that?"

"Stability. It's no secret that her ex has tried to get her back several times. If she gives in because they have a history together, I'd hate for you and Emmie to get hurt."

"That sounds a bit outlandish, don't you think?"

"Is it? I guess you would know best. The last thing Emmie needs in her life is drama. Of course, I'm not telling you something you don't already know."

I gathered all of my things and reached for the handle to the back door.

"The guys are outside working on the cabinets. I'm going to give them a heads up and then head out. If your mother needs anything, tell her to give me a call."

"I'll let her know. Drive safe."

"Thanks."

After filling the guys in, I threw my bags in the back of the pickup and started to head out. I'm sure Lexi meant well, but I never questioned Payton's intentions before now. Yeah, sure, she mentioned that her ex tried to get her back, but up until now, I dismissed it. Concerning Emmie, I've always worked hard to protect her heart after her mother's passing. That would forever remain a priority to me.

A call came in on my Bluetooth. "Hello?"

"Oh, good, I'm glad I caught you on the first try."

"Hi, Mom."

"Hi, dear. I wasn't sure if you'd be busy, but it sounds like you're driving."

"I am. I actually had to leave the job site and head over to the Matthews' really quick."

"Is everything okay?"

"Hopefully, it will be. I'll know more when I get over there.

It appears as though William left the house, and nobody knows where he is."

"Oh, no. Please let me know how everything turns out. I hope they find him soon."

"That makes two of us. Is everything okay with you and Emmie?"

"Yes, I was calling because I'm planning to take Emmie out for burgers later on, and we were wondering if you wanted us to bring something back for you?"

"Mom, did you let Emmie talk you into going out to eat?"

"Absolutely not. I promised I'd take her last week, and I'm not about to break my promise. I'm a grandmother of my word."

I shook my head and smiled at the thought of how much my mother spoils Emmie. Thankfully, she's a rather mature young lady and doesn't take advantage of it.

"Okay, well, you two enjoy. There's no telling what time I'm going to be home, so I'll pick up something on the way in."

"Are you sure?"

"I'm good, Mom. I'll be home as soon as we find Will."

"Okay, dear. Be careful."

"I will."

I drove the next several miles, thinking about what Lexi said to me. In the end, I knew Payton was a woman with good intentions, and Lexi was to be ignored.

By the time I arrived and shut off the engine, Payton and Abby were walking toward the house. I was prepared to do whatever it takes to help get Will home safe and sound.

Payton ran into my arms. I held her as tight as I could.

"Did you cover the whole area?" I said to Abby.

"We covered this entire street, and Payton walked down to the beach. We've literally been door-knocking, and no one has seen a thing. It doesn't make any sense. He has to be around here somewhere. You don't just disappear into thin air."

"I think we should call the police. They can cover more territory and do it a whole lot faster than us," Payton said.

I agreed with her, but I was still determined to search as well.

"Why don't you two go ahead and call the police and wait at the house with your mother. I'm going to hop back in the truck and canvass the surrounding area."

Payton turned to Abby. "I'm going with Cole. Keep your cell phone nearby just in case."

"Okay," she agreed.

We buckled in and started driving down as many streets as we possibly could. Payton looked in between the houses, and when possible, I drove up to the other beach access points just to make sure we didn't miss anything.

"I just don't understand how this could happen. Dad never wanders off."

I wanted to tread carefully and be sensitive to the situation. But I wondered if this had anything to do with his dementia.

"Do you think he may have gotten a little..."

"Turned around or confused?" Payton was thinking along the same lines.

"Yes, of course, anything is possible," she said.

"However, if that's the case, this incident would be a first."

"Maybe we should check the places he would normally go. You know, like his favorite store or the library or someplace like that."

"On foot? That's quite a distance to travel on foot."

"I don't know, I'm just trying to cover all bases."

Payton's cell phone vibrated.

"It's Mom."

I was hoping this was the positive news that we all needed to hear.

"He's where? Yes. Uh-huh. Wow. How in the world did he end up there?"

I pulled over while she listened to the rest of what her mother had to say. When their conversation concluded, Payton looked almost as pale as a ghost.

"Did he make it back home?"

"Not quite. He's at the police station, and we have to pick him up."

"How did he end up there?" I was baffled to say the least.

"Apparently, a man found him walking towards the station. He said he looked lost. When he asked him where he lived, Dad couldn't remember, so the man took him to the police station."

"Wow."

"Yeah, wow is right. The police said dad arrived just before Abby called to file a report. Thankfully they recognized him as the former owner of the Inn."

"Man, oh, man."

The police station was just a minute's drive from where we were. The exterior of the station was under construction, which easily made the place stand out from the road.

Once inside, we made our way to the front desk. Payton seemed anxious to see her dad.

"Hi, my name is Payton Matthews. I'm here to pick up my dad, William Matthews. I can show you my I.D."

I scanned the room, and just beyond the plexiglass, I could see Will. He was sitting in his blue robe, talking to an officer.

"Miss Matthews, we've been expecting you. Wait here, and I'll bring your dad right up."

"Thank you, sir."

I nudged Payton on the arm and pointed her in the direction of her Dad. He had on white knee-high socks and slippers with his robe. He looked very comfortable in his bedroom attire and was chatting it up as if this was a normal occurrence.

"Oh, Daddy." She spoke in a low voice.

The officer brought Will to the front and tried to see if he recognized us.

"Sir, this woman is here to pick you up. Do you recognize her?" the officer said.

Will started smiling. "Do I recognize her? Of course, I recognize her. That's Payton, my daughter. She's my middle child."

I let out a sigh of relief.

"And this fella here is Cole. Cole owns Miller Renovations. You should give him a call sometime if you ever need any work done. He does a great job."

Payton looked puzzled but continued to listen.

"Well, alright, looks like you all passed the test. Miss Matthews, he's all yours."

"Thank you, officer."

She grabbed Will and gave him a tight squeeze.

"Sweetheart, we just saw each other this morning."

"I know, Daddy, but you gave us all a pretty good scare."

"I just went for a little walk and lost track of time, that's all."

"Dad, you do realize I just picked you up from a police station, and you're wearing your night robe, right? Mom is home worried sick about you."

He looked down at his clothing as if he were discovering for the first time what he was wearing.

"Well, I guess we better get home then," Will said.

Payton sat in between us in the pick up as we drove back to the house. We drove in complete silence for a couple of minutes before she started asking questions.

"Dad?"

"Yes, sweetheart."

"Just curious."

"Yes?"

"What were you doing walking around outside in your robe?"

He laughed. "I wish I could tell you. I'm still trying to figure that out myself. It seems like the darnedest thing."

"Yep. The darnedest thing," she repeated.

"The old mind isn't what it used to be. I guess I just forgot." Will stared out the window.

Payton looked at me and I at her as we pulled up to the house.

"And now the real fun begins," she said.

Not quite understanding what she meant, I asked, "What's the real fun?"

"Finding a way to explain all of this to Mom. I barely understand it, so I know she's about to have a cow."

Will let out another chuckle.

"I suppose she will have a cow. It was just a little mishap. Everybody has an off day every now and again." He stepped out of the truck and made his way inside.

It was apparent that Mrs. Matthews was going to have her hands full, keeping an eye on Will.

PAYTON

*A*fter the disappearing incident with Dad, several days passed, and Mom was still nervous. The specialist confirmed that it was the progression of Dad's dementia that influenced the behavior. Mom considered hiring an aid to help out at the house, but Dad refused.

Back at the store, I continued to prepare for the grand opening, which was now two days away.

The bells on the front door rang. It was Cole entering with a cooler and a lunch basket.

"Well, well. Look at you all ready for opening day."

"Do you like it?"

"What's not to like? It doesn't look like you have much left to do."

"Not in terms of setting up, but I'm still plugging in all of the inventory online. Later on, Rebecca is going to stop by and help me with a couple of techie items, and then I should be good to go."

"It's a family affair. I like it! In the meantime, I thought it

SUNSETS AT PELICAN BEACH

would be nice to return the favor and bring you lunch. Please tell me you haven't eaten yet?"

"No, your timing is perfect. I'm starving."

"I had every intention of calling first, but the Donovan project is giving me a fit."

I wondered whether I should take this opportunity to tell him about Lexi.

"What's going on with the project?"

"You know Mrs. Donovan. Just when I think we're making headway, she comes up with a few changes or makes a new request that we didn't plan for. All of which adds time that I really don't have to spare."

I set up our food over by the couch so we could sit down and eat on the coffee table.

"This reminds me that I need to create a space for lunch breaks in the back."

"I'm sure your assistant would appreciate it when you hire one."

In between taking bites of my sandwich, I managed to divert his attention back to the project.

"So, getting back to the Donovans, why don't you just set a hard and fast deadline? Just stress that you have to settle on a final design so that you can adhere to a schedule."

"It sounds easier said than done. I'm trying to move them along, but you know how it is. Even after we're finished, I still have to help out with their fundraiser, so I want to tread carefully while trying not to lose my mind."

"Fundraiser?"

"Yeah, Lexi laid the pressure on to help out with their annual fundraiser, and I caved."

"About Lexi."

I gathered up the nerve to say what was on my mind for quite some time.

"With everything going on, I didn't have a chance to talk to you last week."

"What's up?" he said.

"Cole, I'm almost certain Lexi is trying to drive a wedge between us."

He looked surprised by the statement.

"Are you serious?" He laughed it off.

"Yes, I'm very serious."

"I know she can be a handful, but she would never try to do something like that. What makes you say such a thing?"

To me, it was obvious. But sometimes, men had a way of letting matters like this fly completely over their heads.

"Let's see. Shall we start with my encounter with her last week? I tried to come in and bring you lunch like I normally do, but I couldn't because she was too busy grabbing the food and shoving me out the door."

"Shoving you?" he said.

"Well, not exactly shoving, but she did take her foot and slam the door closed. Which was totally uncalled for."

"She told me you had to run along because it was about to storm."

"See, that's what I'm talking about right there. Yes, it was about to storm, but I tried to come in and say hi. What she was doing was intentional."

"I'll admit she has a way about her, but I'm sure she didn't mean any harm."

If I didn't know any better, it seemed like Cole was defending her.

"Really? Well, I wasn't going to say anything, but to me, it's nothing but a continuation of the way Lexi and her mother treated me when I was working for them."

"What do you mean?"

"Mrs. Donovan made it very clear that she thinks her

daughter Lexi is a better choice for you. And, she didn't mind letting me know face to face."

"Keywords being 'last year'. I'm sure she knows by now that we're together."

"Okay, Cole. It seems like no matter what I say, you have it all figured out."

"Payton, that's not what I meant."

Thankfully, I was finished with my food. I thought it might be a good idea to start cleaning up before the conversation became even more irritating.

"Paytonnn...come on. Don't be like that."

He took the napkins out of my hands and laid them down.

"Come here." His hands slid around my waist.

"Look, the Donovans are long time clients and friends. I know they can be a handful at times, but I don't pay attention to any of that."

"What kind of client or friend tries to come between you and your love life?"

He paused.

"I can't explain her actions. All I can do is assume that Lexi was being her usual irritating self, and it probably just came off the wrong way."

"Well, you know what they say about those who assume?"

I probably was pushing it with the last comment, but my level of annoyance was at an all-time high.

"So, you don't believe me?"

"Cole, of course, I believe you. It's just Lexi and her mother that I don't trust."

"Come here."

"I'm right here."

"Closer," he said.

Cole kissed me. Then he paused to look me in the eyes, draw me in closer, and kissed me again. Being in his arms always made me forget about everything else. Sadly, the sound of the front door opening brought me back to reality.

"Hello, love birds." Rebecca grinned.

"Hey, Rebecca. How are you?" Cole said.

"I'm well, thank you. It looks as if you two are even better."

I balled up the paper bag on the counter and tossed it at her head.

"Payton Matthews, you don't want to start that with me. The last time you threw something at me, you ended up soaking wet."

"That means I still owe you one. Better sleep with one eye open." I teased.

We both inherited our playful spirit from Dad, which Cole found to be amusing.

"You two are funny. Listen, I need to head back, but try not to hurt each other while I'm gone."

He gave me a final kiss before leaving.

"Payton, before I forget. Emmie wants to know if you can come over for dinner tonight. I told her you might be really busy planning for the opening, but of course, she still wanted to extend the invitation."

"I wouldn't miss it. What's on the menu?"

"Whatever my Mom decides to get together. She's watching Emmie until I get home."

"Cole, your Mom deserves a night off. Why don't you ask Emmie if she would like for us to cook together?"

"Me? Cooking? Hey, I already warned you about my cooking a long time ago."

"I know. Don't worry. We'll show you a thing or two. I'll pick up the groceries on the way to the house if you want. Just send me a text and let me know."

"Sure thing. I love you."

"Love you too."

"See ya, Rebecca."

"Bye, Cole."

Rebecca pressed me for information once he left.

"Sooooo..." she said.

"So, what?"

"So, it looks like things are going really well with you two."

"Yeah."

"That's it? That's all you have to say? I'd give it a year tops before the two of you are making wedding plans."

Rebecca had come a long way from being the one who initially had a crush on Cole.

"We're just enjoying each other right now if that's okay with you."

"Yeah, well, don't get too comfortable in that space because I can tell that man is head over heels about you."

"You think so?" I said.

"Yes, of course, I think so. Wake up and smell the coffee, Payton. He waited for you when you were uncertain about dating after the divorce. He dropped everything to come be with you when he found out about Dad, and let's not forget that he has a daughter who absolutely adores you!"

She had a good point. Cole was supportive, and Emmie was very easy to get along with.

"I know." I continued to listen.

"Do you? Because you don't sound so sure."

"I'm sure. I just have so many things on my plate. I guess I lost focus there for a little while."

"Well, whatever you do, don't lose focus on what you have with Cole. Someone will come along and snatch that good man up so fast, you won't know what hit you."

That was the problem. I was very well aware of someone ready to put her claws all over him if given the chance.

"Enough about me, how's everything with you?" I said.

"Same as usual. The workload never ends."

"Do you have time to help me with a few things on the computer?"

"Sure. Oh, I knew I had something to tell you!"

She clapped so loud till she darn near scared me out of my skin.

"You're not going to believe this. I just took on a new case at work. It's a huge deal. Guess who the defense attorney is for the case?"

"Are you going to give me a hint?"

"See if these clues jog your memory. Tall, dark brown hair, Pelican Beach High... prom king and queen."

My mouth flew open in utter disbelief.

"Ethan Davis?"

"Yep!"

"Oh... my... gosh..."

Ethan was Rebecca's high school sweetheart. They were perfect together. Everyone just knew they were going to get married after college. He received a full ride to UCLA, which was great for him, but not good for the relationship. They tried to stay connected after the move, but the distance made it difficult.

"Wow, what's he doing in Pelican Beach? I thought he decided to plant his roots out in California."

"Apparently, he uprooted from California and is now planting his roots in Pelican Beach again."

"No, wayyy."

"Yes, way!"

I couldn't tell if Rebecca was excited or annoyed. One would think they'd be happy to catch up after all these years.

"Why the sour face? I'm sure it was nice catching up, right?"

"Nice? I don't think so. He stood in the courtroom looking like some sort of arrogant hotshot who already knew he was going to win the case. He didn't even recognize me at first. He blew right past me with his fancy suit on looking like something out of a magazine."

She was one to talk. Rebecca was the most competitive, well-dressed lawyer I'd ever met. And I wasn't just saying that because she was my sister.

"So, what did he say when he realized it was you?"

"He finally humbled himself and cracked a smile. I think he was surprised to see me in court, to be honest."

"I don't know why. You always said you were going to be a lawyer from day one."

"Who knows, maybe he was just surprised to see that I'm still here in Pelican Beach," she said.

"Did he look good?"

"I wouldn't know because I wasn't looking at him like that."

"Yeah, right, Becca. Save it for someone who doesn't know you better."

"He looked nice, but I couldn't care less. He showed me how important I was to him after he left for UCLA."

Eventually, I was going to finish working on my inventory. I was determined. But right now, it was clear that Rebecca needed to talk, so I put my pen down.

"That was years ago, Becks. You can't blame him for doing what was best for his education."

She looked away without addressing my comment.

"It doesn't matter. I just thought you would get a kick out of knowing he was back in town and working on the same case."

"I guess it really is a small world." I joked about it, but there is some truth to it.

"Either that or a small town," Rebecca said.

That's something we both could agree on.

"Alright, let's get on the good foot. After I help you out, I'm going to stop by the house and check on Mom and Dad," she said.

"Perfect. That way, I can head to Cole's for dinner without having to worry."

"How's Dad doing this week?"

"He's back to his usual. Nothing out of the ordinary, but I can tell that Mom is not back to normal."

"Understandably so. I'm just thankful that he didn't get hurt."

"I know."

We spent the next couple of hours organizing my online system. It was rare that Rebecca spent much time away from work, so I was grateful for the extra help.

PAYTON

I arrived at Cole's house around six to cook with Emmie. The past year had been filled with opportunities for us to bond. We visited amusement parks, built sandcastles, and even did schoolwork together. As of late, her most favorite thing to do is explore with my camera. She's actually a pretty good photographer.

"Grandma, Payton's here. I'll get the door." I could hear Emmie yelling to Alice from the front porch.

"Payton!" she said.

"Emmie! How are you?"

"I'm good. Do you like my new Converse sneakers?"

"They're too cute. The pink and white matches your headband perfectly."

"Thank you. That was my whole plan."

Emmie recently entered this new phase at eleven years old, where looking cool mattered a lot to her. She didn't like to leave the house with her doll anymore, but secretly she still kept a whole collection in her room.

"And guess what else matches?"

"What?"

"Wallaaaa." She pulled a pink and white polka dot apron out from behind her back.

"Do you like it?"

"I love it. It looks like somebody is ready to cook!"

Alice invited me in.

"Somebody has been ready to cook ever since her dad called and said that you were coming. Speaking of her dad, he should be here any minute now. Put your things down and make yourself comfortable."

"Thanks, Alice."

She always made me feel welcomed whenever I came over.

"Emmie, at your request, tonight's menu will consist of grilled salmon, baked potatoes, and asparagus," I said.

"Delicious!"

"I have to say I'm rather impressed. I thought you were going to say something more along the lines of cheeseburgers and fries."

"I like burgers and fries, but Dad likes it way more. He could eat burgers and fries every day of the week."

"Well, tonight, we're going to show him how to make something different."

Alice confirmed Emmie's confession about Cole's eating habits.

"I don't know where your dad gets his habits from because it's certainly not from me."

Cole walked into the kitchen just in time to join the conversation.

"What's this I hear about my eating habits?"

Emmie thought his timing was hysterical.

"Don't stop now, everybody. Carry on. You were saying something about me eating way too many burgers." He teased.

"You know it's true, Dad."

"I see how it is. I guess next time I'll just have to go to Neil's Famous Burgers all by myself."

"All by yourself? You can't do that.."

"Emmie, don't fall for it. You know your dad is just teasing you," Alice said.

Alice was so cute. She had beautiful white hair, styled in a bob, and always smelled like something sweet. She was a natural when it came to cooking and baking.

"I'm going to let you guys get settled in the kitchen while I get ready to head back to the house," Alice said.

"Aww, Grandma, I thought you were going to sleep over?"

"Emmie, Grandma just spent the last two nights here. I have to get back and check on the house."

"Mom, you could at least stay for dinner."

"Thank you, sweetheart, but I actually have plans. A friend of mind is stopping by the house this evening."

Cole had a curious look on his face.

"Grandma is allowed to have a life too, you know," she said.

Cole didn't look happy.

"Where did you meet your friend, Alice?" I asked

"We met at our last HOA meeting. Turns out, he moved into my subdivision last year, and I had no idea. He's a nice gentleman."

"Does this nice gentleman have a name?" Cole said.

"Yes, his name is Stanley. I'll have to share more with you later, son. I don't want to be late."

The doorbell rang as she was speaking. Emmie and I had already started cleaning the asparagus and preparing the seasoning for the fish.

"You stay here. I'll get the door," Alice said.

When she left the kitchen, I teased Cole about his reaction.

"Aren't you rather protective?"

"Hey, I only have one mother. I'm just doing my job and looking out for her, that's all."

Emmie leaned over and whispered in my ear.

"Dad doesn't like it when Grandma meets new friends."

"Is that so?"

It was all in good fun. I don't think Cole really had an issue with Alice meeting new friends. He just liked to make everyone else think he did.

"Okay, Emmie, where's your Old Bay seasoning?"

"Right here."

I looked up and saw Alice walking into the kitchen with Lexi Donovan. Cole accidentally knocked a bottle of water onto the floor.

"Cole, you have a visitor. Apparently, you left your cell phone at the Donovans' house."

Emmie ran over to hug Lexi and say hello.

"Lexi, you're just in time for dinner," Emmie said.

I could feel my whole demeanor start to shift. Cole glanced at me before responding to Emmie.

"Emmie, honey, that's sweet, but I'm sure Lexi has to head back."

He turned to Lexi. "Thank you for bringing my phone. I must've left it on the counter."

"It's no problem at all. The last time I lost my phone, I completely panicked. I figured you would want yours right away."

"You should've called the house number. I could've easily turned around and driven back."

"Oh, nonsense. As much as you've done for us, it was the least I could do."

Was it unreasonable for me to envision myself dragging her out of the house by the ponytail? Of course, my mother raised me better than that, but a girl could dream, couldn't she?

Everyone in the kitchen fell to an awkward silence before Lexi turned to acknowledge my presence.

"Hi, Payton. I didn't realize you would be here."

"Hi, Lexi."

Emmie continued to try and convince Lexi to stay.

"Please stay for dinner, Lexi?"

"Sure, why not?"

Alice looked confused. If this wasn't a bold move on Lexi's part, I don't know what was. Clearly, she was ignoring the social cues coming from the adults.

Cole spoke up. "Uhh, Lexi, I'm sorry. I know Emmie is excited."

He glanced at Emmie while he continued to speak.

"But, tonight was a special evening planned to spend time with Payton. We're all going to cook together, right, Emmie?"

He gave her a look.

"Right," Emmie said.

"And, since Payton went out of her way to make sure we have just enough groceries and all..."

"I get it. No worries," Lexi said.

She walked over and bent down in front of Emmie to speak to her.

"Emmie, I'll tell you what. How about we plan a special evening soon?"

"Okay!"

"It can be you and me and even your dad if he wants to join us."

I continued shaking the seasoning on the fish. It was probably going to be the saltiest fish I've ever made, but I had to do something to keep from giving this woman a piece of my mind.

"I guess I should be on my way," Lexi said.

"I'll walk you to the door." Cole left with Lexi while Alice stayed back.

"Sweet Emmie, I forgot my purse in the guest room. Would you run and grab it for grandma?"

"Sure, I'll be right back."

Alice stepped closer so that only I could hear her.

"What in the world was that about?" she said.

"Oh, this is normal for Lexi. She's been on a mission lately."

"So, this is not the first time something like this has happened?"

"Nope. Her mother made it very clear to me last year that Lexi is a better fit for Cole. Ever since then, it's been one subtle charade after the other. Except now, it's worse since he's working on their kitchen renovation."

"Well, why don't you say something to Cole?"

Alice's voice died down as he entered the kitchen with Emmie trailing behind.

"Thank you, Emmie," Alice said.

"Give grandma a hug and a kiss. I have to get going before I'm late."

"Love you, Grandma."

"I love you too, sweetheart."

She walked over to Cole afterward.

"Cole, I won't say a word, but I'm sure you already know what I'm thinking."

"I know, Mom. I'm on it."

She gave him a pat on the arm.

"Good. That's what I like to hear. Enjoy dinner, everyone."

Before closing the front door, Alice yelled back to Emmie.

"Emmie Miller, make sure you head to bed early tonight. I'm going to be here bright and early in the morning to take you to your tennis lessons."

"Yes, Ma'am."

Emmie and I resumed veggie prep while Cole cranked up the grill.

"Alright, ladies. I'm an expert at operating the grill, but I still need to learn more about prepping the food. Do you have any tips?"

"For starters, never season the food while you're distracted," I said.

Emmie looked at the fish.

"Looks like Payton poured a lot of seasoning on the salmon. That's okay. We can rinse it off. Don't worry, I know just what to do."

I had to laugh. You know it's bad when an eleven-year-old has to take over in the kitchen.

"Where did you pick up your cooking skills, Emmie?"

"Grandma. She taught me everything I know."

"Well, maybe I could learn a thing or two from you and your grandma."

We wrapped everything in foil and turned the grilling responsibilities over to Cole.

"Thanks for being here tonight. I'm so sorry about earlier. I didn't know she would..."

"It's okay. I know. Just make sure you follow your mom's advice."

We were talking around the subject as not to say too much in front of Emmie.

"Look, guys." Emmie pointed toward the sunset. Watching the sun dip below the horizon was absolutely breathtaking.

"Isn't it pretty?" she said.

"I'm going to get my sketchpad. Hey, Payton, would you like to do a few sketches with me while we wait for the food?"

"I'd love to!"

"Cool, maybe we can sketch the sunset before it goes all the way down. I'm going to get my supplies. I'll be right back."

When Emmie left, Cole took the opportunity to sneak in a kiss.

"I've been waiting to do that ever since lunch."

"You better stop before you get busted." I teased.

"Emmie knows how much I love you. When she pointed out the sunset, a thought came to mind."

"What was the thought?"

"I think this would be a beautiful setting for a ceremony someday."

"Really? What kind of ceremony did you have in mind?"

His face turned a little flush.

"The kind of ceremony where two people come together and publicly confess their love for one another."

Emmie returned with her art supplies. I wanted to respond to Cole but thought it would be best to save it for our alone time. Instead, I kicked up my feet on the deck and began to color with Emmie.

"Okay, this is going to be tricky. I have to leave just the right amount of room on the page for the ocean and the sun setting behind it."

"If you don't get it the way you want the first time, I have plenty of paper," she said.

"Emm, you have a few minutes, and then you'll have to work on the rest of your sketch later."

"Okay, Dad."

"Payton, will you stay for a while after dinner?" Emmie asked.

"I sure will. I never eat and run."

"Good. That way, we can finish our sketch and have girl time."

Cole chimed in. "Hey, since when did this become a girl's party?"

"I'm sorry, Dad. Of course, you're invited too."

She leaned over as we continued to sketch. "We'll have to have girl time on another day, so Dad doesn't get jealous."

I nodded in agreement. Emmie truly was a sweet girl with the biggest heart for everyone she knew.

"Wait a minute. We forgot the baked potatoes," Emmie said.

"Yikes, we sure did."

"No worries. Grandma taught me a microwave trick for potatoes, so technically, we're good."

I showed her my best attempt at a few ocean waves. I was trying, but drawing was not my area of expertise.

"Emmie, it's a good thing we're not entering a contest."

Later that evening, after dessert and more drawing, Emmie retired to her room, and I had to head home. I was down to one day of prep time left before the grand opening, and I wanted to make sure everything was perfect.

"I wish you could stay a little longer," Cole said.

"I do too, but I'll be useless in the morning if I don't get some sleep."

"I'll walk you to the car," he offered.

We walked hand in hand to the driver's side of my car before pausing to say our goodbyes.

"About the whole Lexi thing. I promise nothing is going on between us. Is she being overbearing? Absolutely. There was a long period when I didn't have anyone special in my life, so I really didn't give much thought to her interacting with Emmie."

"Cole, it's clear that Emmie likes her. I don't want to interfere with that."

"Yeah, but it's also clear that Lexi is using it as a way to get under your skin. I'll deal with her. Besides, the job should be winding down soon anyway. Then there's the fundraiser, but I'll find a way around that too."

"Thank you."

"There's something else I wanted to talk about," he said.

"What's that?"

41

"I was serious when I said this would be the perfect setting for a ceremony. The truth is, it wouldn't matter to me if it were here or anywhere in the world. But, I can definitely see myself spending the rest of my life with you. Emmie and Mom love you too. You're a perfect fit for us, Payton."

I didn't know what to say. It felt good to hear, but I was nervous at the same time. There were so many significant changes going on in my life. Last year there was the divorce, moving back home, and meeting Cole. Then there was the whole ordeal with selling the Inn and Dad's health, and now the store. I don't know how many more changes I could handle.

"You seem hesitant. Most people say when you meet the person you want to spend the rest of your life with, you just know. For me, it's pretty clear."

I knew I couldn't just stand there without responding.

"I love you, Cole. You and Emmie and Alice mean everything to me."

"But you're not ready to talk about a marriage yet. I get it," he said.

"That's not what I meant."

He leaned on the back of the car, looking in another direction.

"Cole, please don't do this. We had a wonderful night. Let's not spoil it now. I love you with all my heart. You know I do."

"So, you think that me pouring out my heart to you is spoiling the night?"

"No. I just meant..."

"Don't worry about it."

"Cole?"

"Don't worry about it. Forget I ever said anything."

"Come on, Cole. Are you serious? Can you just put yourself in my shoes for a minute? If you took just a half a second to look at the roller coaster of a life I've had before now, I think you would better understand. I'm not saying no. I just need to think it through."

We stood in silence for another minute. I knew his feelings were hurt, but I was hoping he would understand.

"It's getting late. Send me a message to let me know when you get in," he said.

"Okay."

Cole walked back toward the front porch. There was no kiss and no hug, just a somber end to the evening.

REBECCA

*I*f Ethan and I were going to be working together, I needed to lay down a few ground rules. He was nothing like the guy I knew back in high school. Yet, he was behaving as if we were still best friends who hadn't lost track of time.

I waited until we were alone and told him what was on my mind.

"Listen, we have to lay down some ground rules if we're going to be working on the same case. Rule number one, I'm not helping you, so stop asking me a ton of questions. That's what your legal assistant is for. My job is to defend my client."

"I didn't expect that you would," he responded.

"Good. Rule number two, you will treat me as a professional colleague at all times. I'm not the same Rebecca you knew from Pelican High. Are we clear?"

"Yes, Ma'am."

I grunted at his snarky response.

"Is that all?" he said.

"For now, it is."

"You've changed a lot. The Rebecca Matthews I knew had a little fire and passion in her but was always nice to me. I don't recognize this Rebecca at all."

"What did you expect would happen when you started calling me by my nickname in front of my colleagues? No one calls me Becks at work. You didn't think I would be embarrassed or that people would wonder why you were being so personal?"

"Okay, I'm sorry. It won't happen again."

"You were just showing off. You're trying way too hard to make a name for yourself, but nobody cares, Ethan."

"Rebecca."

"What?"

"I'm sorry."

It was about time he showed me a little respect.

"Can we start over?"

"How?" I said.

"Well, let's start with the basics. How have you been?"

I was way past the point of wanting to have small talk.

"I'm fine, Ethan, thanks for asking. Look, I have to run. I'll see you in court on Friday morning."

I left him standing in the hallway with his briefcase in hand.

I planned to work from home this afternoon, but not before stopping to check on my parents first.

I drove with my convertible top down and the radio playing all the way to their front door. From the looks of things, I wasn't the only sibling who decided to stop by for a visit.

"Hi, Aunt Rebecca."

"Hey, Maggie. Where have you been, girlie? I haven't seen you and Aidan in a while."

My niece and nephew were covering the driveway with sidewalk chalk.

"We've mostly been at the pool every day."

"Come here and give me some sugar."

They gave me a hug and wet kisses before returning to their drawings.

"Is your Mom inside?"

"Yes, she just went to get us some more chalk. She'll be right back."

"Alright. I'm going to go inside to see Gram. Make sure you stay nearby where we can see you."

"Okay."

Abby and I almost bumped right into each other at the door.

"Hey, Abby."

"Hi. Long time no see. Where have you been lately?"

I put my bag down on the couch.

"Working non-stop. Apparently, I'm too busy for my own good. I can't remember the last time I saw the kids."

"I guess it comes with the territory of being a lawyer," she said.

"Yeah, I guess. How's Wyatt?"

"He's pretty good. Thankfully he's been able to adjust his schedule to work from home a couple of days a week, so it's nice."

"I'm going to do the same thing this afternoon. Just thought I'd stop by and see what Mom and Dad were up to first."

"Mom is digging around a few boxes looking for some more sidewalk chalk and Dad..."

Dad walked in while Abby was talking and finished her sentence.

"Dad is ready for his afternoon nap!"

Ever since dad had the incident with wandering away from home, it made me realize just how precious life is. Thankfully, it hasn't happened since then. However, I think everyone functions very differently as a result.

"Dad, you definitely have the right idea. A nap sounds pretty nice right about now. Either that or squeezing in some beach time, which I never seem to get enough of these days."

Abby gave Dad a pillow to use while sitting in his recliner.

"Speaking of beach time. I'm not sure how we all got out of the habit of Saturday morning breakfast and beach time together, but we need to find a way to get it started again," Abby said.

"Somebody pinch me. I must be dreaming. My older sister actually wants to spend time with me?"

"Don't spoil it, Rebecca. I just think it was a nice tradition that all of us had going, and somehow we're letting our busy schedules get in the way. I'd hate for all of us to look back one day and regret it."

"True. I'm sure it's going to be even more difficult for Payton with the grand opening. I have to make it my business to stop by the store tomorrow. I know it's a big day for her."

"She'd like that a lot. We're all going over to show our support tomorrow."

Mom entered the living room with a gigantic bag of sidewalk chalk.

"One large bag of sidewalk chalk coming right up."

"Thanks, Mom. If I would've known it was going to be such an intense search, I wouldn't have said anything."

"Oh, it's no bother. I knew I had some. It was just a matter of remembering where."

She came over and gave me a kiss on the cheek.

"I thought I heard your voice. How's my girl?"

"I'm good. I came to check on you and dad. It looks like he's ready for a nap, and you look like you're buried in chalk."

She looked down and dusted her pants off. Mom was the

kind of grandmother who always kept fun toys and games on hand to keep her grandkids entertained.

"I guess I do look a little dusty."

Abby grabbed a folding chair to take outside.

"I'll be outside with the kids if you need me."

"Okay, dear."

"Rebecca, would you like something to eat?"

"I'm good, Mom. I can't stay long. I'm supposed to be working from home this afternoon."

"Oh, okay. Well, I won't hold you up now, but when you have a chance, I have some legal papers I want to show you."

"Legal papers? Is everything alright?"

"Everything is fine. It's about your uncle's estate. After he passed away a couple of years ago, he left a few things to the family. Anyway, I thought all of that was sorted out a long time ago. I barely understand all the legal jargon, so when you have some time, I'd like to sit down and go through everything."

"I can take a quick glance at it now if you'd like."

"No, no, you need to get your work done. We'll sit down sometime soon, on a day when you're not working."

"Okay, I'll leave it up to you to remind me. On another note, how has Dad been?"

"You know your father, Rebecca." She spoke more softly.

"He still has his days, where he struggles to remember things. He's also as stubborn as a mule, which makes my job more difficult."

"Maybe he's not aware of just how bad it is?"

"I don't know. Some days are good and other days not so much. I'm worried that the latest tests are going to come back with more severe results."

"Really?"

I followed mom to the back, where we could talk more freely.

"I watched his father struggle with the same thing. I'm not trying to speak it into existence, but the behavior looks so familiar. Just keep praying for your father, and let's hope that I'm wrong."

"I will. And, I want you to promise me you're going to remain positive. Besides, it's not like Dad hasn't been to see the doctors before. I'm sure they would've told us if there was something more severe going on."

"Maybe."

Mom didn't seem to be as optimistic, but she did live with Dad and was able to see everything firsthand.

"Don't forget to stop by Payton's place tomorrow."

"I won't. I was just telling Abby that I plan on being there. We certainly have plenty going on to keep us all busy."

"You're right about that, but I look forward to having something to celebrate."

"Me too."

I started making my way back to the living room to pick up my purse.

"I knew I had something to tell you. Guess who's back in town?"

"Who?"

"Ethan."

She thought about it for a minute.

"Ethan Davis. The guy I went to..."

"I know who he is. How could I forget Ethan Davis? I was just shocked, that's all. How is he?"

"Fine, I guess. He's the defense attorney on a case I'm working on."

"Get out of here! What a small world."

"Too small."

"Is he still single?"

"Mom!"

49

"I was just wondering, that's all. Seeing how you two were prom king and queen, and almost destined to be married."

"Okay, clearly, I made a mistake by sharing. I wouldn't care if he was single, married, or otherwise. He walked in that court-room like an arrogant jerk and had the nerve to call me Becks in front of everyone just like it was old times. Ugh. How unpro-fessional."

Mom thought it was amusing. I felt like I could spit fire just thinking about it.

"After all these years, I see he still has an effect on you."

"That's my cue to get back to work. I have a pile of paper-work to go through and a ton of research to do."

She yelled behind me as I made my way to the door.

"Mmm-hmm. Have fun, dear. And tell Ethan I said hi when you see him again."

"I'll do no such thing. Then, he would know I was talking about him."

"So, you care about what he thinks?"

I marched right out of the house. I knew she was just being funny, but the last thing I needed was to be teased about Ethan. I'll admit to feeling raw after he left, but that was so long ago. Now, there was no way he could have an effect on me, no matter how hard he tried!

PAYTON

The first hour of the opening was quiet. My family stopped by to celebrate and dropped off an assortment of cookies to leave out for my customers. As time passed, my excitement was starting to dwindle.

"Honey, give it some time. The whole town knows about your store. We put up fliers, you posted ads, now you just have to be patient and wait. Besides, you have one special visitor who's just walked in the front door."

She pointed toward Cole.

"Thanks, Mom."

I walked over to say hello. It was the first time we'd spoken since our little awkward exchange.

"The store looks great."

"Thanks. Unfortunately, I can't make any money without the customers."

"Don't worry. I saw a few people pulling up in the parking lot. You'll be just fine."

I didn't know what to say. I don't know why I always struggled to embrace the next level with Cole. It's not like I didn't

51

love him. Fear had become one of the side effects leftover from my previous marriage.

"I hope it's okay that I stopped by. I didn't want to miss your first day."

"It's more than okay. I'd be sad if you weren't here. Cole, you know I always let my nerves get the best of me. I didn't mean any harm the other day..."

He placed his finger on my lips.

"I know. I love you, Payton. We have plenty of time to continue that conversation. But, today is your special day, and I just came by to wish you good luck."

He always knew what to say to put my mind at ease.

"Alright, you two. From the looks of things, you have some customers heading this way. We're going to get out of your hair, but before we do Cole, we wanted to extend an invitation to you and Emmie. We're all having a family day at the beach on Sunday. We'd love it if you could join us."

Mom was so excited to invite Cole but forgot to fill me in.

"Hey, what about me? The store will be closed on Sunday."

"Yes, Payton, that goes without saying. You've been so busy this week I almost forgot to tell you."

"Gee, thanks."

Cole laughed. "Helen, I wouldn't miss it. Emmie's going to be thrilled."

"Excellent!"

Mom clapped her hands and gathered up the troops. "Alright, Matthews clan. We better get out of here and make way for Payton's paying customers."

"You guys can't leave without getting a quick family photo out front."

"Okay. Let's hurry up. Rebecca, Abby, kids, family photo out front. And where's Will?" Mom said.

"I'm right here. I was just paying my water bill, that's all."
Dad answered.

"Yikes, Grandpa. Did you have to tell everyone in the whole
store?"

Maggie was sure to call somebody out for saying something
embarrassing. Her younger brother Aidan, was more of the
quiet type and just smirked at his Grandpa.

After a quick family photo that included Cole, everyone
left, except Abby. She agreed to help me out until I was able to
secure part-time help.

My first customer was Mrs. Delaney, who requested a
family photo shoot on the beach.

"I think we're going to go with a traditional theme.
Everyone wearing white tops and either tan or blue bottoms.
What do you think?"

"Go with the tan. Maybe the guys can wear shorts and the
ladies skirts or shorts. It will give the pictures that clean, crisp
beach look that you're going for."

"Perfect. Let's secure a date for that, and then I want to talk
to you about picking out the photo albums. We'll need multi-
ples made for myself, my sisters, and my parents. It's a gift from
Steve and me to the family."

"I have a large selection of albums to choose from. I can
bring out some for you to look through, but I really think you'll
be inspired once the pictures are ready."

"That makes sense. How about we start with the appointment for the photo shoot and go from there?"

"Great, I'll meet you next Thursday at 3:00. I'll call the day
before to confirm the exact location on the beach. Here's my
business card in case you know of anyone else who needs my
services."

"Perfect!"

Abby was taking care of a customer who wanted to

purchase a few frames. For now, the bulk of my business would heavily rely on jobs outside of the store, like weddings, photo-shoots, and private parties. However, it was nice to finally have a place where my clients could come and work on the finishing touches.

The bells on the front door rang, and Mrs. Donovan walked in. If I had known she was coming, I would've put up the 'closed' sign. *Look what the cat dragged in,* I thought to myself, but wouldn't dare say it out loud.

"There she is. Payton Matthews... what a cute little place you have here."

Even Abby could tell this woman was not a welcomed guest.

"Mrs. Donovan, how are you?"

"I'm well. I came to see what all the fuss was about. A little birdy told me today was your grand opening."

"Yes, it is."

She looked around while dangling her purse on her forearm.

"Surely, a grand opening should be overflowing with more customers."

"We just had a few customers. I'm sure there will be more. How can I help you today?"

"I don't really need anything. I just figured I'd come and show my support for your opening day. I have to get back to the house soon. Cole is finishing up, and I asked Lexi to take care of him."

Abby rolled her eyes and went back to helping the other customer. I had just about enough of the Donovans and decided to defend myself once and for all.

"Did you drive all the way over here to congratulate me or to rub it in my face that Lexi is alone with Cole right now?"

"Well, perhaps a little of both."

The audacity of this woman. I don't think in all my years I've ever come across someone so brazen.

Abby's eyes bulged wide open. I lowered my voice and walked from behind the counter.

"Mrs. Donovan, thank you, but I can assure you that I don't need your well wishes. Since today is Cole's last, I can tell you what I've really been thinking. I'm not intimidated by you or Lexi as you so desperately try to lure Cole in for his affection. In case you hadn't figured it out, we actually keep an open line of communication. There's no amount of clothing you could send to Emmie, no amount of begging for him to pencil you in his schedule, and no amount of pleas for him to participate in your fundraisers that could entice Cole to date Lexi."

I might have said more than I should've, but what was she going to do? Run back to the house and tell Cole? I don't think so.

I returned to my usual tone.

"It was so nice of you to stop by. Let me escort you to the door."

"I can see my way out, thank you."

She turned beet red and grunted as she left the store. If I had known it was going to be that easy, I would've talked to her a long time ago.

My other customer was leaving. "You have a lovely store. I have a friend who just recently got engaged. I'll pass your card along to her."

"Aww, thank you!"

"Have a great day," she said.

"You too."

When I turned around, Abby was holding up her hand to give a high five.

"I'm so proud of you for putting her in her place. What a slithering snake."

"Was it that bad?"

"No, it was that good!"

"Abby, you're crazy."

"I honestly didn't know you had it in you. That seems like something I would do, not you. After everything you've told me about those two, she had it coming."

"I think I felt more empowered after talking to Alice the other day. Even she was turned off by Lexi's bold ways."

Abby was right. The Donovans had been wreaking havoc for a long time. Hopefully, today's conversation nipped things in the bud once and for all.

We had several customers stop by, and at least ten more photo shoots lined up. It was a good start for the first day, and I was looking forward to many more good days to come.

PAYTON

*F*amily beach day had finally arrived. The first few days of the store's opening was a hit. Some family time on the beach was very much needed, and I couldn't wait to work on my tan. My niece and nephew were digging around in the sand with Emmie. The women were perched under their umbrellas with their guys by their side, except for Rebecca.

Abby's husband, Wyatt, began teasing Rebecca about a sensitive subject.

"Rebecca, how come you didn't invite the prom king to the beach today?"

All ears were listening for a response...

"Wyatt, now you're asking for trouble," Mom said.

Rebecca sat up in her beach chair, looking like she was ready to put her boxing gloves on.

"What did you hear?" she said.

"I didn't hear anything. I've just seen him around the court-house lately, so I assumed he's back in town. You forget I was already dating Abby when you two were an item in high school. I remember your prom night like it was yesterday."

"That's right. Wyatt was at the house the night of your prom," Abby said.

I slid my beach hat over my head. I had this funny feeling the conversation was about to head south real quick.

"Good ole Ethan. Wasn't he supposed to help us with cutting the grass?" Dad said.

I think Dad was getting Rebecca's former boyfriends mixed up. Even though who could blame him. She definitely had her fair share to choose from over the years.

"That's the wrong guy, Will. We're talking about Rebecca's prom date from Pelican High." Mom helped Dad to follow along.

"Go ahead, Rebecca. Tell them how the two of you have reconnected recently," Mom said.

"We haven't reconnected. We're just working on the same case together, that's all."

"Now that is funny. Out of all the lawyers to work with, the two of you get assigned to the same case?" Cole said.

I tried to silently warn him that he didn't want to get involved. Rebecca was liable to chop all their heads off for finding any humor in the matter.

"Wyatt... Mom... and Cole... I'm glad you all find this funny, but there's nothing more to it other than the case. That's it."

"So there's no chance the two of you, who both happen to be single, were assigned to the same case for a reason? Maybe it's fate," Mom said.

"Fate my foot. We know absolutely nothing about each other. We've both changed, and that was a long time ago."

"Well, on that note, I'm heading down to the water. Who's with me?" I said.

Cole kicked off his shoes and volunteered to join me.

"Emmie, I'm going to take a walk with Payton. I'll be back."

"Okay, Dad."

We walked hand in hand down to the ocean. Cole was glistening from his suntan lotion. But more than his amazing looks, I was proud of the way he got along with the family.

He playfully flickered some water at me.

"Cole Miller, you better stop before I toss you into the ocean."

"Impossible. We both know who will go down first." He teased.

Knowing that I wouldn't stand a chance at dunking him in, I surrendered.

We continued walking along playfully like two teenagers in love.

"I think we might've hit a sore spot with Rebecca," he said.

"We're good. It would've been worse if we stayed there and continued to participate."

Cole laughed.

"Do you think she still likes him?"

"He's having some sort of effect, but it's hard to tell with her."

Cole picked up a seashell and began writing in the sand. The message read 'Cole loves Payton.'"

"I know someone by the name of Payton Matthews, who's having an effect on me."

I loved how transparent he was with me.

"I'm sorry I made you uncomfortable the other night. I was just trying to express my feelings toward you. Perhaps I should've kept it simple like the message in the sand."

"No. You did exactly what you were supposed to do. And if you ever stopped being that transparent with me, it would break my heart. I wanted to kick myself later on that night. I realized that I was choosing to let fear get in the way of my biggest blessing, which is you."

"Really?"

"Really! I love you, Cole. I've never had a love like this before. Sometimes I freak out when I'm about to embark upon something new. But that's all it is... just a brief moment where I feel like I'm losing control. When the moment passes, and I let go of trying to be in control, my heart always returns back to where it needs to be."

"Which is where?"

"It's with you," I said.

He picked me up and twirled me around.

"So, does this mean you're actually okay with the conversation we were having the other day?"

"About the ceremony? Yes. I'm more than okay with the conversation. I think we should explore the topic whole-heartedly."

"Whoooooohooooo," he yelled.

"You would've thought I just said I do, Cole."

"It feels like you just said I do in my heart. Of course, I want to do this the right way. We can talk about it more later on. Just know, in my heart, I have every plan to give you the kind of life you deserve."

I couldn't hold back the tears any longer. For years I felt like I was pretending to be the wife of somebody who didn't love me anymore. I was doing the right thing, trying to keep my vows, even though love had left our home long before the divorce. And now look... it's amazing how all of that was changing right before my very eyes.

"Don't cry. Your family is going to think I said something to upset you."

"Oh, they're all the way over there. They don't know what's going on. Besides, these are happy tears."

"I'll take happy tears any day." He rested his arm around my shoulders.

"Come on, let's go check on the kids."

The kids designed a beautiful sandcastle. Beside it, I caught a glimpse of Aidan's head sticking out of the sand.

"Aunt Payton, come rescue me. They buried me in the sand."

"Oh, boy. Looks like they're playing a game of two against one," Cole said.

"I wouldn't fall for it. He might be the youngest, but somehow, I think he was a willing participant."

"Good point."

Later that afternoon, Cole headed back home with Emmie, and the rest of us went to my parents' house to eat. Wyatt introduced us to his new barbecue recipe, while Mom made whipped cream from scratch for the strawberry shortcake. It felt like old times sitting around and enjoying each other's company.

"When are we going to get back to our weekly tradition? We can't keep making excuses about how busy we are. If Saturday mornings don't work anymore, how about Sunday afternoon? Everyone is here now without a problem," Abby said.

Mom gave Abby the thumbs up. "I agree. Having time with my girls is nice, but having everyone over has been a real treat as well. Plus, I think it's good for your father. He needs to be more active and less worried and distracted."

Rebecca gave Mom a squeeze and then sampled the whipped cream. "That applies to you as well, Mom. It's good for both of you not to worry so much."

"Worry is my middle name," Mom said.

It was obvious where I inherited my habits from.

"Girls, while I have you all here, there's something I've been meaning to share with you."

Mom walked over to the kitchen drawer and pulled out a piece of paper.

"I started to share this with Rebecca the other day because it's rare that we're all together at the same time. However, this pertains to all of you, and I'd like for you to look it over."

"Is this the legal document you were talking about?" Rebecca said.

"Yes. It was years ago that you all had a chance to meet your great uncle on your father's side of the family."

I remember we had a great uncle, but I don't recall us being very close.

"Well, turns out after he passed away, he left his property in Savannah, Georgia to his daughters."

"What does that have to do with us?" I said.

"Hold on. I'm getting to that part. His daughters, unfortunately, couldn't care less about the property, and don't want to have anything to do with it. From what I understand, it's overgrown and is in dire need of TLC. They want to honor their father's wishes not to sell it and to keep it in the family. At least one of his daughters has continued to pay the taxes so they wouldn't fall behind, but she's ready to pass the place onto someone else."

"Again, I'm confused as to what this has to do with us?" I leaned back on the kitchen counter, feeling a little anxious about the whole thing.

"Payton, you know I don't like to leave out details. Give me a minute. I'm getting to that part now."

Mom held up a document that said quitclaim deed at the top.

"The daughter, who's been keeping the taxes current, recalls that your great uncle was very fond of your father. He used to talk about Will and his three daughters all the time. I'll admit there was some truth to their bond because your father would always make time to talk to Uncle Samuel. And on occasion, he would go out to visit him whenever he could get away from the Inn. Anyway, the daughter remembered their bond and wants to turn the property over to you if you're willing to accept. All of the paperwork, plus a detailed letter explaining everything, is right here. Both sisters are ready to sign off on the property."

"What? No way. Who does that?" I said.

I couldn't believe what I was hearing. Most people that I know would sell the property for a profit and call it a day.

Rebecca started looking through the papers to verify what Mom was saying.

"Well, I'll be. There may be some truth to this, after all," she said.

"The property has to be a piece of junk if both of them are willing to give it up so easily. Think about it. Why else wouldn't they have sold it by now or bought the other one out?" Abby rolled her eyes.

I didn't think it was a good idea at all.

"I'm not sure what's going on with the property, but I wouldn't be so quick to sign those papers. The last thing I need is something else major to think about when I have a new store to run," I said.

"Well, you're not the only one who has to think about it, Payton. All three of our names are on this document. I think it's worth looking into." Rebecca tried to make a case, but I wasn't buying it.

"You can count me out as well. I'm not interested in taking on someone's fixer-upper several miles away," Abby said.

"Hold on. Don't be so quick to jump the gun on this, Abby. Why don't we start by looking up the property address online? I'm sure one of the realtor websites will have a little information about the potential value. It's not one hundred percent reliable, but it's a start."

"Girls, slow down a minute. This letter is clear that the new deed would be made out to the three of you, not just Rebecca. I suggest you make a few calls and get the details. Then decide from there."

"I don't care if it was a lake house in Charleston or a mansion on a hilltop somewhere. The fact that they've just abandoned the place and it's overgrown as Mom described is enough for me to wash my hands of it all. It sounds like too much of a headache for me. I have the kids and Wyatt to think about. I'm good." Abby pushed in her chair and left the kitchen.

"Does Dad know about this?" I wondered.

"I mentioned it to him, but he didn't have much to say about it," Mom said.

You could tell that Rebecca had an attitude.

"Great. Whenever it seems like there's the slightest chance we can collectively get along, Abby starts her nonsense." Rebecca started gathering her things.

"Don't put this on Abby. You're missing the big picture. This is a joint decision. One that you seem very excited about without having much information."

"There you go defending her. This might be an excellent opportunity for us. And maybe it's not, but you'll never know if the two of you are going to dismiss it before we have a chance to check it out."

I shifted my focus back toward the barbecue and all that was good in my life. I didn't want any part of our great uncle's property, and I certainly didn't want sibling drama.

LEXI

*M*om and I couldn't be more pleased with the arrangements for the fundraiser. We had a variety of auctions to bid on and games for the children to play. Local business owners and residents were arriving at the fairgrounds in droves. The only thing that would make this day even more special was seeing Cole. He confirmed he was coming, but I hadn't seen him since he finished my mother's kitchen.

"Lexi, don't look now. Cole is coming with Emmie and Payton." Mom warned.

"That's interesting. I don't recall extending an invitation to Payton."

"I didn't think you would. Just put on your game face and act as if you couldn't care less."

"Will do."

Mom started walking over to greet them.

"Cole, it's so good to see you."

"Hi, Mrs. Donovan. You remember Emmie and Payton?" He placed his hand on Emmie's shoulder.

"Yes, sweet Emmie. It's been a while since we've seen each other. Your Dad talked about you all the time when he was working at my house."

"Hi." Emmie spoke and then ran over to give me a hug.

"Payton."

"Hello, Carol."

"I decided to bring the whole crew with me. I figured since it's a fundraiser, the more, the merrier," Cole said.

"Payton, how's business treating you these days? You must not have many customers if you have time to be here today."

"I have plenty of customers to keep me busy. Thankfully, my sister is looking after things so I could be here for a couple of hours."

She looked up at Cole, and he smiled back in a way that showed how much he cared for her. Maybe it was time that I let the whole thing go. My mother meant well, and I agreed with her for a long time. But today it was hitting me like a ton of bricks. Cole was making a choice to be with Payton. Who was I to stand in the way?

"There's no sense in all of us standing here. We have work to do if we're going to raise money for the children. Emmie, how would you like to help out at the cotton candy booth?" I said.

Emmie perked up. "That sounds awesome."

Mom continued to look as if she had a chip on her shoulder, as I tried to urge everybody to get going.

"Cole and Payton, feel free to take your pick about where you want to volunteer. I know the dunking booth is off-limits, but just about all the booths could use an extra hand."

"No problem. And before I forget, here's our donation."

Cole handed over a generous check which Mom gladly received. When they walked off, Mom approached me.

"You feeling okay? You seemed rather friendly and accepting of Payton's presence."

"Mom, you know I love you," I said.

"Lexi, I love you too. I just want what's best for you."

"Cole Miller is not what's best for me. I think we both know it. Look at him."

She glanced over at Cole, who was still walking hand in hand with Payton.

"He's head over heels in love with her. I want somebody who loves me that way. What we're doing... it's not right."

I walked away to give her time to think about what I said. When the time was right, I got Payton's attention to have a private conversation.

"Hey, Payton, do you have a minute to take a walk?"

"Lexi, I didn't come here for any drama. I'm just here to..."

"I know. I actually just wanted to say I'm sorry."

She looked at Cole, who encouraged her to come and hear me out. We strolled past some of the kids playing games and made our way to an area where we could talk.

"You deserve an apology from me. I've been giving you a hard time, and you don't deserve it. I'm sincere when I say that I'm sorry."

Admitting I was wrong was difficult, but it was time to correct the error of my ways.

"Thank you, Lexi. I have to admit I'm a bit surprised. You and your mother haven't been fond of me for a while now."

"Yeah, well, that stops today. Mom just wanted what she thought was best for me, and I went along with it. Who wouldn't want a good guy like Cole? For the longest time after Laura's passing, there was no one in his life. She thought we would be a good fit and I didn't disagree. Then you came along, and I didn't think it would last. It doesn't matter what I thought or what my mother thinks. What matters is that Cole is happy with you. "

"Wow, I don't know what to say, Lexi."

"It's okay. You don't have to say anything. It's not like I expected you would want to be friends or anything. I just wanted to do the right thing and apologize."

She hesitated for a moment. I probably would too if I were in her shoes.

"I accept your apology," she said.

Payton extended her hand to me. It was a start to a civil existence, which is all I could ever ask for. I didn't know if I'd ever find my happily ever after, but if I did, it definitely wouldn't be by sowing seeds of discord.

We returned to the booth where Cole was working.

"Everything okay?" he said.

"Couldn't be better. Thank you again for coming out and being a part of the fundraiser. I hope you two have fun and don't forget to help yourself to something to eat."

"Thank you," Payton said.

"Absolutely. I'm going to check on the other volunteers. I'll see you later."

I blended into the crowd feeling good about the choice I made. Sometimes a change in attitude was all you needed to help set you on the right course.

REBECCA

$\mathcal{T}$he case I was working on with Ethan was short-lived. The charges were dropped due to tampering with evidence. This created a no-win situation, and my client was set free. Thankfully this also meant that I didn't have to work with Ethan anymore.

When the court was adjourned, he followed me to the elevator.

"Rebecca. Rebecca, slow down."

I kept walking, hoping the elevator doors would open in time.

"Hey, slow down."

I pressed the lobby button and turned toward him.

"Let me guess. You're disappointed the case was dismissed because you didn't get to do a victory lap."

"We all know the odds were in my favor with this case, but that's beside the point."

"Whatever, Ethan."

"I'm just kidding with you. Come on, lighten up. Why are you being so hard-nosed with me?"

I'm not sure I had an answer to that question. I mean, how ridiculous would it sound if I confessed I was still annoyed at something he did over twelve years ago?

"I'm not being hard-nosed with you. I just don't think we have much to say after all these years."

"How would you know that if you don't give it a try? I, for one, would sincerely like to know how you're doing," he said.

"That's funny. You didn't seem to care about that while you were at UCLA, or while you were starting your big-time law career." I lowered my voice, so I didn't draw attention.

"What do you mean, big-time law career? Last time I checked, we both work at the same place."

"Yeah, well, at least I remained loyal and dedicated my time to giving back to our home town."

"So, now I'm to blame because of where I chose to go to school? Come on, Becca. What's this really all about?"

The bell signaled for the elevator to open. I didn't say anything until the doors closed behind us, and we were alone.

"You're not to be blamed for anything, Ethan. The past is water under the bridge. You should just leave it where it belongs."

"You still have feelings for me, don't you?" he said.

"The nerve! Aren't you full of arrogance and pride? I oughta..."

"You oughta what?" he said.

"Oooooh!"

I could feel the steam coming out of my pores. How dare he talk to me that way.

"Some things haven't changed, Becca."

"Call me Becca one more time and see what happens."

"Rebecca. Some things haven't changed. You still get angry as ever when somebody is telling you something you don't want to hear."

The elevator opened, and someone joined us from the second floor. I was relieved because it temporarily silenced Ethan. When we reached the main lobby, I had the pleasure of being followed out to the parking lot.

"Rebecca, hear me out once and for all. If you don't ever want to speak to me again afterward, I'll respect your wishes."

I stopped at the car door.

"You have sixty seconds."

"Okay... I was caught between a rock and a hard place. What was I to do? I was eighteen years old and received a full ride to a school that could help open doors for my future."

"I wasn't upset with you for choosing to go to UCLA, Ethan. Look at you. Still clueless after all these years. I was upset with you for losing touch with me. I know we were young, but I loved you. I checked my email and even my voice-mail to see if I had a message from you. But eventually, you just stopped reaching out. That said a lot about how much you cared."

I felt as if I was reliving the sadness all over again.

"Not so. I stopped because I didn't want to hold you back from meeting someone who could be there for you."

"What? All you needed to do was keep the lines of communication open. I would've waited for you," I said.

"How could I expect you to wait for me? You were smart and beautiful and one of the most popular girls out of our senior class. I knew you were going places with your life. Was I really supposed to expect that you would wait around for me?"

"It doesn't matter, Ethan. I feel like we're beating a dead horse at this point."

"It does matter. I admit I was wrong for the way I handled things. I see that now. But please don't hold that against me forever. I swear on everything I have that I wanted what was best for you. You can even ask my parents. My mom used to send me care packages because she knew how upset I was about being apart from you. She used to beg me to call you, but I knew that wouldn't change the fact that I couldn't be with you. I genuinely felt that you were better off without me."

For the first time, I realized there was another side to the story. Back then, I always felt as if I was the only one who cared.

He continued explaining. "I used to ask mom about you all the time. Occasionally when she ran into you, she would update me. After a while, I think she stopped on purpose because she could tell it brought back painful memories."

His words knocked the wind out of me. "I didn't realize you were impacted."

"Well, I was. I know that was a long time ago and you've moved on with your life. But as I stand here looking at you, it feels like it was just yesterday that we hugged goodbye for the last time. Some wounds take longer to heal more than others, and some never heal."

I couldn't believe what I was hearing.

"You were my high school sweetheart. Most high school sweethearts get married. That's what should've happened with us. If I wasn't so young and dumb about how I handled things, we'd probably be married today," he said.

"That's a little presumptuous, don't you think?"

"Is it? Ask anybody, and I bet you they'd say the same."

He was probably right. I dated after Ethan but never loved anyone the way I loved him.

"I guess we'll never know," I said.

"Never say never. I followed you out here to see if there's any chance you'd be open to a fresh start at getting to know each other again?"

"Ethan, we're a little too old to play high school sweethearts, don't you think?"

"I'm not proposing that we play anything. The least that can come out of it is the chance to catch up on old times. The best that could come from it is an opportunity to finish what we started. Either option is much better than how we left off. Wouldn't you agree?"

He always had a way of making me crack a smile even when I didn't want to.

"Agreed."

I caved in. Let's face it, spending time with Ethan couldn't be any worse than hanging out with the guys I'd met over the years. At least I was more familiar with this one.

"Alright. Now we're talking. If you would be so kind as to write your number on this..."

He rummaged through his briefcase, looking for something to write on.

"What kind of lawyer doesn't have paper in his briefcase?" I teased.

"Oh, this whole briefcase and fancy suit thing is just for show. After all, I do have an image to uphold as a hotshot lawyer. I think that's what you called me, right?"

"Ha... ha... ha. Now I'm going to call you Ethan, the comedian."

"I'm just teasing ya."

"Good. Besides, you don't need a pen. I have the same cell phone number that I've had since senior year."

"Are you serious?"

"I guess there's only one way to find out."

I winked at him before sitting in my car and turning over the ignition. When I put my window down, he leaned over to share a few parting words.

"I hope you're telling me the truth. If not, I know where your parents live."

"Like I said... there's only one way to find out."

I put my sunglasses on, reversed out of the space, and waved. I didn't foresee this conversation with Ethan turning out the way it did. His desire to reconnect definitely slipped under my radar.

PAYTON

"*P*icture Perfect, how may I help you?" Abby answered.

Abby helped to keep the store afloat while I conducted my last interview for the day. Having her around as things started to pick up had been a lifesaver. However, she needed to get back to the kids, and I needed extra help, pronto.

I brought my interviewee over to the couch to have an informal chat.

"Natalie, thank you for joining me today."

"Thank you for having me, Ms. Matthews."

"Why don't we start off by you telling me a little about yourself."

"Sure, I'm in my junior year of college. My major is in marketing, and I currently have a 4.0 GPA. Since I have a pretty flexible schedule, my plan is to work part-time to start gaining some experience."

Natalie had golden-brown hair that was elbow length and a smile that lit up the room. She wore a very professional looking outfit, and I could tell she was taking the interview very seriously.

"That's fantastic. So technically, this would be your first job?"

"My first job working for someone other than a family member or a neighbor. I used to babysit, and during the summer, I worked at my uncle's hardware store before he retired. It was at the hardware store that I learned the basics of customer service and how to operate a cash register. I can provide references for you if you'd like."

"Wonderful. Natalie, that's just the kind of experience I'm looking for. As you know, my photography store is still rather new. The busiest time of the day for me is afternoons and Saturdays. I need someone who can work the cash register, answer phone calls, and book appointments. Does that sound like something you'd be interested in doing?"

"Yes, that would be perfect. If you hire me, you won't be disappointed. "

I really liked her confidence. So far, out of all the other candidates, she was definitely a strong consideration.

""I love your enthusiasm. I have one last question for you before we conclude. Tell me about a time when you were challenged by a situation at work and how you decided to respond."

"That's a good question. It would have to be the time a customer yelled at me for not finding what he needed fast enough. He was asking for a specific kind of nail that was impossible to locate. I tried my best, and even apologized. Needless to say, he still left the store without his nails."

"That's exactly what I'm looking for. You can't always please everyone. You tried your best, and that's all you can ever do."

"Thankfully, my uncle thought the same thing. I thought for sure he would be mad at me, but he wasn't."

"Natalie, I'm impressed with our interview today. I'm going to reach out to your references and if everything pans out, you should hear back from me by the beginning of next week. How does that sound?"

"It sounds great. Thank you for allowing me to interview," she said.

"The pleasure was all mine."

When Natalie left, I waited to hear feedback from Abby.

"Well, what do you think? I know you could hear us talking from across the room."

Abby didn't seem as enthusiastic.

"She seems sweet and all but, meh," she said.

"Seriously? I think she's a great fit. She's in school, she gets good grades, which tells me she's responsible, and she has experience with customer service. What more could I ask for in a part-time assistant?"

"I wouldn't discount her. But you will have to start this process all over again as soon as she graduates."

"Abby, if that's your only reason, I can live with it. I could say the same for any part-timer. I'm not offering a full-time career. If that were the case, then I'd have to consider someone else."

"True."

"What about the older retired gentleman that you interviewed this morning?"

"No way. He spent most of the time telling me what days he couldn't work because of this club or that club. He didn't sound like he had enough time for a job. Honestly, I like Natalie. I had a good vibe with her. I think we'd work well together."

"If that's the case, then you have your answer. I know Wyatt will be happy to hear you found someone. He's about to lose his mind trying to juggle the kids while they're on summer break, and he's working from home."

"Aww, poor thing. I'll have to treat him to something nice to say thank you."

"Hey, Payton, not to change the subject, but isn't your coo-coo clock supposed to you know, coo-coo? I haven't heard a peep out of that clock since you opened the store for business."

"Haha. You're right, but what was one to expect from a clock that came from a second-hand thrift store? It keeps the time, and it looks cute. What more could a girl ask for?"

I started sorting through various backdrops that were delivered in the mail.

"Do you need help?" Abby said.

"Sure, if you could just help me open each box, remove the backdrop, and then break down the boxes, that would be great."

"My goodness. I didn't realize people use these things in their pictures anymore. I thought folks were more into taking their pictures in the great outdoors."

"They are for the most part, but occasionally, I still have a special request here and there. I just want to be prepared. Not everyone comes in here for a family photo shoot. I had one woman who wanted some professional shots for a modeling portfolio. Another guy wanted something simple for his brochures. You just never know."

"The last time I stood in front of a plain canvas backdrop was probably for my elementary school pictures."

"Oh, man, those pictures are a hoot."

"Tell me about it." Abby continued unpacking boxes.

"Those were the good old days," she said.

"Speaking of the good old days, wouldn't it be nice if we could go on a family vacation again?"

"That would be nice. I think mom could use a break. I know Wyatt and I could use one. I'm not as confident about traveling with dad right now, and I'm sure mom would say the same."

"Yeah, you're right. I'm dreaming more so than anything else, but it would be nice."

The idea of dad's health taking a turn, and my parents not having a chance to do all the things they dreamed about in retirement, made me feel sad.

Abby continued. "I know who would be ready to travel in a heartbeat."

"Who?"

"Rebecca. Except it wouldn't be for vacation. That girl is on a mission to rehab that old, dilapidated house."

"Abby, stop! You stop talking about your sister like that."

The way she said it was so funny she had me in stitches.

"I'm telling the truth about *our* sister, and you know it. I don't know what's gotten into that crazy little head of hers. I have two young little kids, and you're about to become Emmie's step-mother, and you run a business."

"Wait...what?"

"Oh, don't play dumb. You know that man is going to ask you to marry him."

"Abby, you must know something I don't."

"I promise I don't know any more than you do. However, it doesn't take a rocket scientist to figure out that he's in love with you. Now, getting back to the topic at hand. You don't have time, I don't time, and none of us have the money," she said.

"You know Rebecca has always been an ambitious go-getter."

"That's all well and good. She just needs to figure out a way to go get the house on her own. If there's any way my name can be removed, she can have at it."

Good grief. Where would the Matthews sisters be without a tad bit of drama and a healthy dose of spice? I guess it's what added flavor to our family dynamic. Regardless, I loved my sisters and didn't know what I would do without them.

Later that evening, I wrapped up things at the store. I was thankful for another day's work and even more thankful for a text from Cole that read, "Meet me at sunset for a romantic walk along the beach."

"Hello, Mr. Romantic."

I did as he instructed and met him on the beach just a few feet away from his backyard. He gave me a peck on the lips and reached over to take my sandals out of my hands.

"Hello, Beautiful. I'll carry these for you."

"Thank you."

"Come. Walk with me. Tell me about your day."

I could feel the tension of the day releasing as we walked. I exhaled.

"Was it that bad?"

"No, not at all. It was a good day. There's just nothing more relaxing than being out here and listening to the waves and enjoying the sunset with you."

He put his arms around my shoulders, and we continued to walk.

"Okay, about my day. I conducted more interviews this morning, and I think I found my new assistant."

"Congratulations!"

"Thank you. Even though it's not official yet. I still want to check out her references, but her name is Natalie, and she was my favorite by far."

"That's awesome."

"What about your day? Anything special happen?"

"Uhhh, I wouldn't say special. More like difficult. I started working with a new client today who is... get this... even more particular than Mrs. Donovan."

"Noooo."

"Yes! Except in this situation, the husband and the wife both have strong opinions about what they want, and they don't see eye-to-eye."

"Oh, boy."

"Oh, boy is right. But enough about work. I miss you so much; I just had to see you."

"Cole Miller, we just saw each other two nights ago, and we're going to see each other again tomorrow at my parents' house."

"And that's still not enough," he said in a playful voice.

He picked me up, threw me over his shoulders, and started running towards the water.

"Say you're sorry, or I'll toss you in."

"I'm not sorry." I laughed uncontrollably.

"I'm giving you one last chance. Say, Cole, I'm sorry. I want to see you every single day." He was so playful.

"Okay, okay. I'm sorry, I want to see you every single day."

He returned to dry ground and put me down on the sand.

"Good. Now come here and give me a kiss."

I don't think I could ever get tired of Cole's embrace. It always felt right. It was exactly what I needed.

"Turn around," he said.

He turned me toward the sunset, kissed me on my neck and held me from behind. Tonight's sunset was the most tranquil blend of pink and yellow I had ever seen.

"How's that for a view?"

"It's stunning. Absolutely stunning."

We stood watching the sunset and listening to the crashing waves.

"Payton?"

"Yes."

"Is it okay to finish our little talk? About the future."

I turned to face him.

"I was hoping we would."

"Emmie's been asking a lot of questions lately. She's very discerning. I've been honest with her about my feelings for you, but I find myself holding back on the one thing I really want to say most."

"What's that?"

"I want to tell her that I'm ready to ask for your hand in marriage. I know she would be thrilled. She adores you. But in order for me to have a serious conversation like that with her, I need to make sure you're fully on board with the idea as well."

"I'm fully on board with the idea," I said with confidence.

"Really?"

"Yes, really. You two mean the world to me."

He picked me up again and spun me around.

"I'm going to do this the right way and give you a proper proposal."

"Cole, you know I'm a simple kind of girl. Remember our first date? I was the one who brought flat shoes and put them on before we arrived at the restaurant."

"Your definition of simple is beautiful to me. And just because you prefer simple doesn't mean you don't deserve the very best. Alice Miller would never forgive me if I didn't do this the right way. Now, enough about that. Come here and give me a hug."

I prayed that night that our love would always remain this strong. I hoped we would always love each other faithfully and beyond measure, dream the unthinkable, and reach what was previously unreachable. I was looking forward to what life had in store for us.

COLE

*E*mmie and I have been admittedly spoiled by my mother over the years. Ever since Laura's passing, she's made it her business to watch Emmie and cook dinner on my late nights. As a widow, she says it's always given her something to do. I had a big task in talking to Emmie about my plans to marry Payton. Somehow, I knew it would be just as important to have a conversation with mom too.

I made arrangements to come home early to talk to them.

"Hey, Dad. I think grandma is going to be really surprised that we're cooking something healthy for her tonight."

"Is this another joke about my burgers?"

She laughed at me.

"No, silly. I'm being serious."

"I know. If it weren't for you and Payton showing me how to make your special salmon dish, we would probably be eating burgers."

"We wouldn't because grandma would definitely have something to say about it."

"You're right. You know her well, Emmie. Speaking of your grandma, where is she?"

"She's still resting. She should be up soon. Every day around this time, she goes upstairs to have a little rest and trusts me to be responsible. She says that girls need their beauty rest, but I can't fall asleep, so I let her rest for both of us."

"That's cute, Emm, but somehow I don't think it works that way."

I shuffled around in the refrigerator to see what I could find.

"While grandma's resting, would you like to help me prep the food?"

"Sure. How about I take veggie duty, and I'll help you when it's time to season the fish?" Emmie was a natural.

"Sounds like a plan, Stan."

"Who's Stan?" She said.

"It rhymed. Plan...Stan... get it?"

"That was corny, Dad."

"What's the matter, you don't like my jokes? I have more where that came from."

"Oh, boy. How about we focus on the seasoning? Don't pour too much. Remember what happened to Payton when she accidentally spilled extra seasoning on the fish?"

"I sure do, but I also remember you saving the fish with your handy rinsing trick."

"Yep."

Emma passed along the seasoning and started to pull the vegetables out of the bin. If left to her own devices, I was one hundred percent certain she could cook this meal better than me.

"Hey Emms, I actually wanted to ask you about Payton."

"Is she coming over for dinner again?"

"Not this time. We'll see her on Sunday when we go over to Mrs. Matthews' house."

"Cool. What do you want to know?"

"I was wondering how you feel about Payton? You know, as far as your relationship is concerned."

"It's great."

"I'm glad you feel that way."

"I was thinking about changing up the vegetables. Instead of asparagus, why don't we try peas and carrots? It's grandma's favorite," she said.

"If it works for you and grandma, it works for me, honey."

Emmie gathered up the vegetables that she had already washed and returned them to the refrigerator.

"What's wrong, Dad? You seem so serious."

"Oh, I don't mean to be, sweetheart."

She returned with the new vegetables, but instead, I felt compelled to finish my thought all the way through. I don't know why I was so nervous. I kind of felt like it was now or never.

"There's something I want to tell you, Emmie."

"Okay."

"You see, the things is... you know Dad loves you so much, right?"

"Of course."

"And you know that will never change, right?"

"Dad, you're acting mighty strange. We all love each other. You love me, I love you, we love grandma, and we all love Payton."

I was so thankful she added Payton's name in there I almost didn't know what to do with myself. If that was a sign from heaven, I was going to run with it.

"Yes, exactly, Payton as well. And because I love Payton, I was thinking about asking her to marry me. But I didn't want to ake such a big decision without including you. Just like I always promised."

"Well, duh, Daddy. Everybody knows how much you love Payton. Me and grandma have been waiting for you to pop the question."

"Really? No way. Why didn't you say something to me?"

"I dunno. Grandma says these things happen when the time is right. I figured it was up to you and Payton to know when the time was right."

"Emmie, you're so mature. If I didn't know any better, I'd think you'd been here before."

"You say that all the time," she said.

"That's because it's true. So just to be certain, you're okay with the idea of Payton being your step-mom? You can be honest with me. I know it's a big deal."

"I like the idea this much." Emmie expanded her hands as wide as she could.

"Come here, Emms. Give your Dad some love."

I could feel my eyes welling up, but I tried to hold back.

"That makes me so happy to hear. I know Payton loves you so much."

"Can I be in the wedding?"

"I don't see why not. Of course, we should probably talk about it with Payton as well."

"Yeah, I think that's a good idea."

We both sniggled.

"You wanna hear something pretty strange?" Emmie said.

"I'm all ears."

"I recently had a dream that you and Payton were getting married. But that's not the strange part. The strange part is there was another lady there on your wedding day. She was more like an angel with wings. You could tell she was happy you were getting married because she was smiling. She was like a nice angel."

"Did she look like anybody you know?"

"She kind of had blond hair like Mom does in all of her pictures. But I couldn't see any other details. It was just a really nice dream, and I was sad that I woke up."

"That's the sweetest dream I've ever heard."

"If Mom is watching over us, I think she'd be very happy that you're getting married. I also think she'd be very happy that you found someone like Payton to be my new step-mom."

Emmie gave me a big squeeze. I was thankful that at eleven years old, she wasn't too old to have a heart to heart with her Dad. I knew I was biased, but I thought she was a pretty amazing kid if I say so myself.

"I was thinking we might want to talk to grandma about this tonight at dinner. What do you think? Would you help me?"

"Sure. But for now, if we don't start cooking, there won't be any dinner."

"Good point, young lady. Let's get started before grandma wakes up."

"Maybe if we can get everything in the oven in time, we can make dessert," she said.

"Emmie Miller, you're pushing your luck. Unless there's ice cream in the freezer, you know I can't bake."

"We'll figure something out." Emmie shook her head and laughed at me.

Later that night, we talked things over with my mom. It turns out she was just as candid as Emmie when it came to wondering when I would pop the question. Women are pretty discerning about these things. Now that everyone was on board, the only thing left to do was talk to Payton's parents, and plan the proposal of a lifetime.

REBECCA

*E*than invited me to meet him at the beach for an afternoon stroll. He said he wanted to catch up, so we met near the Inn that my parents used to own.

"I can't believe you actually showed up," he said.

"I don't see why not. I'm the one with a track record of keeping her word, remember?"

"Touche, touche. It's just that all the way up until the other day you weren't so fond of me. I was hoping you wouldn't have another relapse and change your mind."

"Makes sense. I think anyone in my shoes would've been sore about the way you left things. However, I'm not going to keep harping on it."

"Thanks. I know I can't make up for lost time. But, I invited you here because I'm genuinely curious to know how you've been. How's life treating you?"

I watched my red toenail polish disappear and reemerge as we walked in the sand. It was my way of finding something to focus on instead of looking at him too much.

"Life has been pretty good. After our senior year, I went to college, determined as ever to get my law degree. There were a few times when I wanted to quit."

"That doesn't sound like you. You're not a quitter."

"It didn't turn out that way, but it was tough. The course work was hard, passing the bar was a nightmare, but my biggest challenge was having to prove myself. I was thrown right in the shark tank with a bunch of arrogant male lawyers who assumed I didn't know what I was doing. Trust me. It was an uphill battle."

"I'm sorry you had to go through all that, but you made it. Who's the hotshot now?"

"If you say so. I still have to prove myself, no matter how experienced I am. And I'll do it till the day I die because I refuse to be mistaken for one who can't pull her weight."

"I don't think anyone could ever think that about you, Rebecca. I watched the way you handled yourself in the courtroom. You were no-nonsense. Even I was afraid to mess with you."

"You should've been."

Ethan smiled at me.

"What?" I said.

"Nothing. Keep going, I'm listening."

"I don't know that there's much more to tell. I still live in Pelican Beach. I bought a house about five or six years ago. It gave me the space and privacy that I needed, but yet it's close enough to family. I'm a workaholic, but I'd like to think it's helping me stay on my A-game, and it helps me fine-tune my craft."

"Boring!" he said.

"Excuse me?"

"You shouldn't center your whole life around work. Don't get me wrong, be thankful that you're blessed enough to have a job. But there's more to life than just work."

"Like what? What do you do outside of work that's worth talking about?"

"Well, one of the reasons I moved back here was to be closer to my family. I missed out on a lot of precious time with them by living in California after school. I can't get the time back, but I can start being more intentional about spending time together before it's too late."

Ethan was right. Our folks were growing older, and the family dynamic had changed over time. Looks like he had more depth to him than I was initially giving him credit for.

"Then there's my personal hobbies. I like to play golf to help me unwind. It's kind of fun getting out there and working on improving my game whenever I have some downtime."

"That's nice."

"Do you have any hobbies?" he asked.

"Not really. I like to work out to relieve stress. That's about it. Lately, I've been thinking about getting into property investment, but for now, it's just another avenue I'm exploring. Nothing really definitive."

"That's the go-getter, I know. Lawyer by day and real estate mogul by night."

"Now that you put it that way it sounds exhausting just thinking about it."

"I bet you it is exhausting." He teased. "If you don't mind me asking, are you seeing someone?"

Ethan picked up a shell to trace in the sand as he waited for my response.

"No. My options are looking kind of scarce these days."

"You're kidding me. The guys used to follow you around Pelican High like you were a celebrity. To this day, I'm surprised that I ever had the privilege of calling you my girlfriend. You could've easily chosen to be with anyone. What happened?"

"Your guess is just as good as mine. Perhaps I'm too independent, or too much of a go-getter. I'd like to think one's success wouldn't influence their relationship status, but I don't know."

"Maybe you just haven't met the right one."

"Now you sound like my mother. She's always talking about how he's out there preparing himself for me. And how I need to be focused on becoming the best me I can be for him. That sounds good and all, but the bottom line is marriage may not be for me. Sometimes you just have to be willing to accept the facts and call it what it is."

"Interesting," Ethan said.

"What's interesting?"

"I've battled with similar thoughts, especially with the possibility of remaining single because I haven't met the right one. However, my version is slightly different. I like to think more like your mother. She's out there, it just has to be the right timing. Everything I'm experiencing during the "in-between" time is preparation, that's all."

"Do you think you'll be saying the same thing if you're still single ten or twenty years from now?"

"Guess I'll have to cross that bridge when I get to it."

Ethan kicked a bit of sand over my feet in a playful manner before suggesting that we take a walk to grab something to drink.

"So, tell me about how things are going with the family. Do your parents still own the Inn?"

"Sadly, they sold it last year. My parents had to retire. Mainly due to my dad's health."

"Is he okay?"

"At the time of his retirement, he had what they considered to be early signs of dementia. It's progressed since then, so of course, my mom is always worried."

"Man, I'm sorry to hear that."

"Thanks, he still lives at home with Mom. Some days are better than others. He refuses to allow her to get extra help, and at this point, mom still listens. I often wonder how long they can keep that up, but for now, it works."

"Please give them my regards. I always felt like your family was my family. Your parents always welcomed me like I was one of their own."

"They sure did."

My parents never stopped loving Ethan and always hoped he would return home. If I'd let her, mom would go on and on about how wonderful Ethan is in her eyes. The family had a deep affection for him and treated him like he was one of the Matthews.

"As for my sisters, I'd say they're doing rather well for themselves as well. Payton opened a new photography business recently. It's just a few miles from here. And Abby stays at home with my niece, Maggie, and my nephew, Aidan. Her husband, Wyatt Holden, works in our building. You may have come across him a time or two."

"The name sounds familiar. I think I remember Wyatt. Wasn't he and Abby there at your house the night of our prom?"

"Yes, they were as a matter of fact. You have a pretty good memory."

"Are you and Abby still at odds all the time?"

"I'd like to think we've learned how to get along better, but sometimes we still have our moments. Hey, for somebody who's been gone a long time, you sure did remember a whole lot."

Ethan was like the kid you grew up with since elementary school who knew everything about you and could tell all of your family stories.

"How could I forget?" he said.

I refrained from saying anything further but our bond was

so tight. I wondered how he could just leave it all behind. We grabbed a couple of cool beverages from a nearby stand before he walked me back to my car.

"So, what are the odds that I might see you again?" he said.

"The odds are very high. We work in the same building, remember?"

"Come on, you know that's not what I meant."

I knew what he meant, but I wasn't convinced that hanging out with Ethan was a good idea for my emotional well being.

"I'll think about it," I said.

He stopped walking.

"Seriously?"

"Yep. You'll have to take it or leave it."

"You were always one to drive a hard bargain. Let me guess. You don't want to be seen around town with me? You're probably afraid it will stir up something?"

"No. I'm just not certain I want to give you an immediate yes. At least it's not a no."

He took a sip of his water.

"Good point. I told my mom you were going to give me a hard time."

"You told your mother we were meeting today?"

"Sure, why not? She was so excited to hear that we had a chance to reconnect. You know she'll never stop being fond of you."

Hanging out with Ethan felt just like old times. We fell right back in synch as if we hadn't missed years of being together. That made me nervous.

"Guess who I ran into the other day?" he said.

"Who?"

"Do you remember Tommy Sacks?"

"The kid who used do weird things like eat mud pies when everybody dared him to?"

"That's him. He owns an auto shop on the north side of Pelican Beach."

"Really? How's he doing?"

"He appears to be doing very well. He's married with kids, and best of all, it looks like he survived all of those disgusting dares."

We laughed and carried on some more about Tommy's dares until we arrived at our cars.

"It's a wonder that kid didn't have to make any visits to the E.R." he said.

"I know, right?"

Our laughter trailed off and we found ourselves in an awkward moment of silence.

"Well, here's your car, and I'm parked right behind you."

Ethan tapped on the hood of my car.

"This was nice. Thanks for inviting me," I said.

"The pleasure was all mine. Do you have big plans for this afternoon?"

"Not really. I'm going to swing by Payton's store and see what she's up to. I need to talk to her if she's not too busy."

"That's nice. Well, enjoy the afternoon, and if you should ever change your mind about going out again, I hope you call me."

"Bye, Ethan."

I waved goodbye and drove off. It was hard not to spend the entire drive thinking about our afternoon get together. Who would've ever imagined in a million years that I would go anywhere with Ethan again? Now, the real question I had to ask myself... would I go out with him again?

When I arrived at Payton's, there was barely enough room to get in the store.

"Excuse me. Hi. Coming through. Hi. Excuse me."

When I made it to the counter, a girl stood behind the counter, looking frazzled and overwhelmed.

"Welcome to Picture Perfect. How may I help you?"

"Hi, is Payton here? I'm her sister, Rebecca."

"Hi, Miss Rebecca. It's nice to meet you. I'm Natalie."

I extended my hand across the counter.

"Natalie. You must be Payton's new assistant."

"That's me. Payton is in the back, finishing up a photo shoot. She should be out soon."

"Great, do you need help out here? It's looking kind of crowded."

"They're all apart of the same party. They took a group photo, and now Payton's just working on the last individual photo."

"Oh, okay, that's great. It looks like business is booming. How's the assistant role working out for you?"

"So far, so good. I still have a lot to learn about placing orders and organizing inventory, but overall I'd say it's going pretty well."

Payton returned and announced that everyone's photos were done. She was such a professional. I don't think I've ever seen Payton, the businesswoman in action, but the role suited her well.

"Rebecca, I didn't know you were here."

"I just got here. Natalie and I were getting acquainted while you were taking your last picture."

"Natalie, Rebecca is my youngest sister. She's by far the craziest of the bunch, so don't listen to a thing she says or pay attention to anything she does," Payton said.

Natalie stood there looking uncertain about what to say.

"Thanks, Payton. Now I know how you really feel about me."

I pretended to put my head down and cry just to play

around with Natalie. Poor thing looked at us both like we were crazy.

"Natalie, we're just joking around. Lighten up, girl," I said.

"Speak for yourself, Becca. You might've been joking with the fake crying, but I'm serious about you being crazy."

Natalie finally cracked a big smile.

"Is that how you treat me in front of your new assistant? I'll remember this moment."

"Quit goofing around, Rebecca. What brings you by here today?"

"I was hoping I could talk to you for a little bit if you weren't too busy."

"Sure, why don't you come hang out in the back with me so I can multi-task."

She checked in with Natalie. "Call me if you need anything, okay?"

"No problem," Natalie said.

I pulled up a stool in Payton's back room and put down my purse.

"So, what's on your mind?"

"Where do I begin?"

"Uh, oh. That doesn't sound good."

"It's not terrible. I just have a lot to think about these days."

"Well, are you going to tell me about it, or are you going to just sit there?"

"Okay. Let's start with the most recent event."

I decided to share my thoughts even though I knew I would probably regret it later.

"I just left the beach before I came to see you."

"I thought you looked a little rosy on your cheeks." Payton was digging in her filing cabinet while listening.

"I was at the beach with Ethan."

She stopped what she was doing.

"How did that happen?"

"What do you mean, how did it happen? He invited me to hang out to catch up on things, and I accepted his invitation."

"So, you went on a date?"

"No. I wouldn't call it a date at all. We met at the beach. Took a stroll, talked for a little while, and left."

"Okay, so a semi-date."

"Payton, come on."

"Okay, okay. You don't have to be so uptight about it."

I balled up a piece of paper and flicked it at her but missed.

"First of all... you have terrible aim. Now, can you get back to telling the story? How was the conversation with Ethan?"

"Surprisingly, it was nice."

"You mean to tell me you didn't try to bite his head off? I'm impressed."

"Today was more of an opportunity to catch up, that's all. He knows that I wasn't very fond of the way he left things between us. But honestly, that was so long ago. It seems a little ridiculous to carry on about it now."

"Oh, so this is the second time you're getting together?" Suddenly Payton didn't seem to be as interested in her filing cabinet.

"Not really. The first time he followed me out to the parking lot at work, but we're losing focus here. The main point is we talked about everything, he explained that he never meant to hurt me, and we had a chance to get past that and just catch up. That's it."

"No, Ma'am. That's not it. If that were it, you wouldn't be sitting here at my place of business, telling me you have a lot on your mind. It sounds like you're intrigued by the time spent with Ethan, and you just don't want to admit it."

"It's not like we spent a long time together. I was just

surprised at how easy it was to talk to him. Just as if we never lost time together."

"I would imagine it's because the two of you were always best friends. That kind of bond is hard to break."

"Yet, he still managed to break it," I said.

"Rebecca, he was young. I could go on and on telling you all the reasons why he made the right choice, but I think deep down inside, you know that already."

"So, what are you trying to say?"

Payton walked over and placed her hands on top of mine.

"I'm saying if he's back, and the two of you want to spend time catching up, just enjoy the journey. Life's too short to be stressing over every little thing."

After returning to her filing cabinet, she added, "Besides, what are the odds the two of you would still be single after all these years?"

The last comment was cause for me to make another paper snowball and throw it at her. I realized there may be repercussions for doing so, but what kind of younger sister would I be if I didn't stir up a little trouble?

"Rebecca, will you quit! I'm only going to allow you to be back here with me if you can be civilized so I can get some work done. Now, what else was on your mind besides Ethan?"

"You're not going to want to hear this, but I'm sharing anyway."

"I'm listening," Payton said.

"I followed up and did some research on the property in Savannah."

"And?"

"Turns out the property sits on eight acres of land. It's a cape located on Grove Point Road. It has about five bedrooms with a total of 4,000 square feet."

"Okay." Payton still didn't seem excited.

"I was able to get in touch with a neighbor who was good friends with Uncle Samuel. He says his family keeps an eye on the company that cuts the grass. Apparently, one of the sisters is paying for basic yard work to help keep up the appearance of the neighborhood."

"What about the condition of the house?"

"He said the house needs a lot of work. Upon first glance, it looks like a lovely home from the road, but when you get closer you can see greenery growing out of the gutters, it needs a new roof, and it smells like mold on the inside."

Payton perched her eyebrows. "Great. And you want to take this on as a fun project?"

"I don't know how fun it would be, but I know it would be rewarding. I called a realtor after just to learn about the neighborhood comps. The realtor seems to think this house could easily sell for 750,000, and maybe even higher if it's renovated properly."

"Rebecca, am I missing something here? I thought the whole issue for the daughters is they didn't want to take on the project, and they wanted to honor their father's wishes of not selling the place?"

"That's right," I said.

"Well, the way you're talking, it sounds like you're looking to fix up the house to sell it. Isn't that going against Uncle Samual's wishes?"

"The clause states that we would have to keep and maintain the property for a minimum of five years. Afterward, we'd be free and clear to do as we please."

"Oh, for goodness, sake. No. I'm sorry, Rebecca, but I think we'd be biting off way more than we can chew. It sounds like too much of a headache if you ask me."

"The house is paid for, Payton. Do you realize what we could do with a 4,000 square foot property located on eight sprawling acres of land? Who cares if we have to keep it for five years. We could rent it out. Maybe even target high-end renters and hire a management company to keep the place up. Or maybe we could even turn it into a bed and breakfast. I can just see it now. A small-town B&B located in Savannah, Georgia. I get excited just thinking about it."

I held up my hands imagining a beautiful sign on the front that read 'Small Town B&B' or 'Matthews B&B.'

Payton looked irritated.

"I'm starting to think you've lost your marbles, Rebecca. This is no different from when we were little kids. You always had all of these amazing ideas, you'd get everyone involved, and then would be the first one ready to move onto the next thing once you were bored with it."

"Name one time that happened, Payton."

"Where shall we begin? There was the time you were going to start your Herbal Care business. That was a hoot. No one could tell you anything. You had all of us going around town, putting up signs to order your products. That was short-lived when we found out that hanging up the signs was against the town ordinance. Then, you bribed Abby and me to drive you to your multi-level marketing meetings. You used to come out of those meetings all pumped up and ready to sell products by the box load. All of that quickly came to an end when you realized just how difficult it was to climb the MLM ladder."

"I was nineteen. All teenagers think they have everything figured out. I was very consistent and responsible before that point. You're just not giving me any credit."

"Oh, yeah? What about school fundraisers? Once again, Rebecca comes home all pumped about winning a brand new bike as the first prize. I can still hear you today. "I'm going to outsell every kid at school... weeks later, Mom and Dad were stuck trying to figure out how to get rid of forty plus boxes of assorted candy bars."

"Okay, Payton, you've made your point. The one thing you seem to be forgetting is that I finally grew up and made something of myself. I don't think becoming a successful lawyer is anything to overlook."

"You do have a successful career. But the way you're acting over this whole property thing reminds me of the old Rebecca that gets excited about an idea without giving it a lot of thought. As I stated earlier, I don't have the money or time to be involved in something like this. Neither of us can be in Savannah to properly oversee everything while managing our lives here in Pelican Beach."

"I have given this a lot of thought. There are people we can hire to ensure things run smoothly."

"Rebecca, I don't know how many other ways I can tell you that I'm not comfortable with the idea."

"I didn't expect you to be comfortable with the idea immediately. I'm just asking you to continue being open to hearing the details. Tomorrow I was hoping all three of us could talk through it at Mom and Dad's house."

"I have to get back to work," Payton concluded.

Convincing my sisters to get on board was proving itself to be a lot harder than I thought.

PAYTON

Sundays had become our new family day, which now included Emmie and Cole. We set up a volleyball net on the beach near my parents' cottage. It was fun watching Cole and Wyatt engaging the kids in a few rounds while the women sat on the deck to talk.

"Mom, do you think you could ever live somewhere else besides Pelican Beach?" I asked.

"I don't think I've ever considered it. Your father and I have lived in this town for so long I can't imagine living anywhere else."

"You're in a dreamy location. I would give anything to be right on the beach," Rebecca said.

Mom nudged Rebecca with her elbow. "You didn't do too bad for yourself, Rebecca. Your home is lovely, and you're not that far away. Your only problem is you work so much you don't get to spend enough time enjoying it."

I wondered if what Mom was saying was sinking in for Rebecca. Even she recognized that Rebecca didn't have time to do anything besides focus on her career. How on earth would she be able to take care of a renovation in Savannah?

"Is there room for me to join you, or is this a ladies-only affair?" Cole joined us from his game of volleyball, and I gladly pulled out the chair next to me.

"I have a seat waiting right here for you. Who won the game?"

"Technically, Wyatt and I won, but we allowed the kids to have the final victory," he said.

Emmie ran over and sat beside me.

"Emmie, guess what?" I said.

"What?"

"I was thinking we should have a special date for you, me, Maggie, and Aidan to hang out soon. How does that sound?"

"That would be awesome! Maybe we could go for milkshakes or go swimming or maybe both?"

"I like the way you think. Milkshakes, swimming, or both... hmm."

I turned to Cole.

"What do you think? Does that work for you?"

"It's your call. I'm just jealous I'm not invited," he said.

Emmie took out her dad's old cell phone, which she carried around for fun.

"Payton, as soon as you name the date, I can put it on my calendar."

"Oh, wow, okay. How's next weekend?" I said.

"That works for me!"

She truly was the sweetest kid ever. I didn't know how I got to be so lucky to have Emmie and Cole in my life.

Dad slid the screen door aside and joined us outside. Abby followed behind him with a tray of snacks.

"Hi, Dad. How are you?" Rebecca said.

"I'm pretty good. I just had my mid-day nap. It doesn't get any better than this."

Dad positioned himself to take a better look at Emmie.

"Well, who's this fine young lady?" he said.

"Hi, Mr. William. It's me, Emmie. Don't you remember me?"

"I think so."

Dad looked at me to be sure, so I nodded in agreement.

"It's nice to see you, Miss Emmie," he said. He mosied over to find a place to sit in the shade.

"Whose birthday are we celebrating today?"

"No birthday, Dad. It's just the family getting together to eat." Rebecca rearranged herself to sit closer to him.

"Hey, Dad, do you remember our great Uncle Samuel?" she said.

While they talked, Abby continued to set up the snacks and threw a dagger my way. I knew she didn't want to hear Rebecca bring up the property.

"Good old Sammy. I have to give him a call."

"He's no longer with us, Dad."

"He's gone?" he said.

"Yes, he passed away. But he has a home in Georgia that his daughters want to give us. I was wondering if you ever had a chance to visit his house? Or if you remember him saying anything about it?"

Mom perked up to listen to his response.

"Yes, I've been to his place. It's been many years, but if I can recall, it was a big place. I used to wonder why he had so much land but hardly anybody to share it with."

"Oh, so you do remember?" she said.

"Yes, I remember. I need to give Sammy a call." He repeated.

"Dad, Uncle Samuel is no longer with us, remember?"

He looked at Rebecca and fell silent.

"Your father is right, Rebecca. He always used to get on your great uncle's case about living on all that land by himself. I guess his daughters never had an interest after they grew up and moved out. His wife passed away several years earlier. Sometimes it's hard to leave a place where you have so many memories. It would be nice if whoever takes over the house can restore and maintain it's original character."

Cole rested his hand on my knee. "You didn't mention anything about inheriting property in Georgia."

Rebecca and Abby were waiting to see what I would say.

"It's not an inheritance. We're being gifted the property. Me and my sisters would have to sign the deed together. The reason why I didn't mention it is because I don't plan on getting involved."

I should've filled him in on the details later. I could see Rebecca positioning herself to get ready for round two of this daunting conversation.

"Cole. You're the perfect person to weigh in on this," she said.

Abby cut her off. "Rebecca, don't start. Can't we just enjoy a family day without you imposing your agenda on us?"

"It's our agenda, and I think Cole could give us some wise advice, Abby."

Rebecca proceeded to share the details of the property with Cole. She covered everything from the square footage, the taxes, and even her business ideas. He patiently listened. I secretly hoped he would say something to put this silly idea to rest.

"So, what do you think, Cole?" she said.

"I hear the enthusiasm in your voice. However, I think it would be a tall order to take on something like this without actually being there to oversee things. Even if you lived in

Savannah, the first thing I would caution you about is who you hire to do the renovation work. You want quality craftsmanship at a good price. Nobody wants to be ripped off. Now imagine trying to ensure that you're getting what you paid for from a distance? No bueno."

"But what if I were to make arrangements to check in on the project frequently?"

Cole shrugged his shoulders. "It's not impossible. But would I do it? No."

Abby interjected. "Thank you for talking some sense into her, Cole. Maybe now we can finally put this to rest," she said.

"No, we can't. Where there's a will, there's a way. I respect your advice, but what I really hear you saying is to make this work somebody would need to be there to supervise, right?"

She turned to Cole for clarity.

"That's one major aspect. Of course, there are other things to consider. If you were just talking about flipping the house, that would be one thing. However, if you're bound to keeping it for a certain time, and you want to turn it into a business opportunity, that's a whole other ball game."

"I'd be willing to let go of the business ideas. At a minimum, we should acquire this property and keep it among us to sell in five years for a profit. If not, we're just throwing money away. The house has a zero balance on the mortgage. And it's worth well over a half a million in value. It's a no brainer."

Abby raised her voice. "You're not even taking into account how much the renovations would cost. Wait, here's another logical thought... have you even seen the place in person yet? No! It could have an oak tree growing right through the living room floors for all you know. I can just see it now. We all arrive to see the house for the first time, and you look at us and say something simple like, 'I didn't know it had an oak tree growing through the floor.'"

"Abby, the kids can hear you." I tried to encourage Abby to calm down, but as usual, Rebecca had already pushed the wrong buttons.

"Mom, where did you put the contract? I want to read it over one more time," Abby asked.

"It's in my stationery drawer in the kitchen."

Abby stormed off to get the paperwork while Rebecca rolled her eyes.

"I hope I didn't say the wrong thing. I just wanted to give you honest advice about how I would approach this, Rebecca. If you ask a contractor, they're going to tell you whatever you want to hear just so they can make money."

"Thanks, Cole. I know you're just trying to help. I'm taking what you said into serious account. I just think there are ways around it, and I wish my sisters would get on board."

Abby walked back out on the deck with the paperwork in hand.

"Here's what I think about this letter, the deed, and anything else associated with this house."

She ripped the papers in two. "Now, have I made myself clear?"

"Are you crazy?" Rebecca said.

"Crazy to listen to any more of this foolishness."

I held my head down and massaged my temples. I should've known this was leading nowhere good. It had been a while since Abby and Rebecca had a major disagreement. I just wished it didn't have to be a full-on performance in front of Cole and Emmie.

"Cole, how about you help me round up the kids so we can all prepare to wash up for dinner?"

"Sounds like a plan," he said.

Thankfully the kids were caught up in a game and didn't appear to be paying much attention to Abby and Rebecca.

Rebecca took a deep breath. "Abby, I'm going to be the bigger person and ignore what you just did. Instead, I'd like to propose an idea that would make this nice and easy on all of us."

We waited for her to continue.

"I'll have a letter drawn up to present to Uncle Samuel's daughters. It will clearly state that the two of you are not able to accept their offer, but you're willing to turn the house over to me if they agree to make the necessary changes. The only thing I would need from the two of you are your signatures on the letter. Agreed?" she said.

"I agree. Just provide me with a copy of the letter, and I'll gladly sign," I said.

We all turned and looked at Abby. I love my sisters, but the two of them were as stubborn as mules and tough like bulls.

Mom being the peacemaker, took Abby by the hand. "What do you say, dear?"

"I'll sign the letter if it means we can be done with the topic once and for all."

"Great. I'll have the letter ready by midweek and will take over from there," Rebecca said.

Mom seemed relieved. "Oh, thank God. The last thing I ever wanted is for there to be any strife between you three," she said.

I know they were still irritated with one another, but at least the whole thing was smoothed over for now. Rebecca is so independent and strong-willed. Always ready to take on the world and crush anything that gets in her way. At times I think that bothers Abby. If I know right, Rebecca was going to figure out a way to flip that house. Even if it meant doing it all by herself.

COLE

On Monday, I returned to Helen and William's house counting on Payton to be at the store. Helen and I made prior arrangements for us to talk privately with Will. It may seem a little old fashioned, but I planned on doing things the traditional way. Today I was going to ask them an important question that would impact the rest of my life with Payton.

"Cole, we've been waiting for you. Come on in."

Helen gave me a warm hug and always made me feel like family.

"Hi, Helen. How are you today?"

"I'm pretty good. Follow me, Will's in the living room sitting in his favorite recliner."

She announced my arrival to Will.

"There's my guy. Make yourself comfortable over here on the couch. You're just in time to catch the sports line up," he said.

"William Matthews, Cole didn't come here to participate in your afternoon rituals. He wants to talk to us about something else."

She grabbed the remote and lowered the volume to a decibel that was more suitable for talking.

"I can't seem to peel him away from his daily routine no matter how hard I try. Every day it's the same. Wake up, get dressed, eat breakfast, and then fall asleep while reading the newspaper. In the afternoon repeat the process, except he's already dressed and instead of the newspaper, it's sports. Deviating from the routine is completely out of the question." Helen laughed.

"Well, I won't take sides, but yesterday it seemed like Will did a fine job of deviating to spend time with the family."

"You're right, Cole. I'll give him that much. William has always been the kind of father that puts family first."

Will continued to sit in his chair and listen but wasn't as talkative. It's one of the things I started noticing first as his dementia started settling in. Surprisingly, I felt a little nervous and thought it would be best to get down to the reason for my visit.

"Speaking of the family, I thank you for having Emmie and me over yesterday. It's been nice to be apart of the Matthews family gatherings. I know Emmie would agree with me if she were here."

"It's our pleasure. We love you guys." She glanced over at her husband.

"Isn't that right, Will?"

He agreed. "Yes, dear."

"We love you too. Which leads me to why I'm here today."

We were interrupted by the sound of keys unlocking the front door. Payton came in with a few bags in hand. Helen and I hopped up quickly and tried to act natural.

Payton looked surprised.

"Cole, I thought that looked like your truck out front. What are you doing here?"

I tried to think fast, but Helen answered on my behalf.

"He came to help me with the kitchen sink," she said.

"The sink? I just used the sink this morning before I left for work, and everything was fine. What's wrong with it?"

"I was cooking breakfast for your father, and I don't know if I got something stuck down in the disposal or what. I called Cole because I figured he could recommend someone. Being such a gentleman, he came over to take a look at it himself."

Payton hesitated.

"You left work to come over here and fix the sink?" she said.

"Yeah, I wasn't far from here. I figured since it was my company that installed your parents' entire kitchen, it was the least I could do."

"That's right, you did the renovations for the cottage, silly me. Mom, next time, call me. I could've lined up a plumber to come out in no time."

"It really wasn't a bother," I said.

Payton gave me a kiss and walked over to the counter to lay the bags down. Helen was using her best form of sign language to express that she didn't know Payton was coming home. We stopped mouthing back and forth to one another just in time before Payton turned around.

"Cole, if I would've known you were going to be here, I would've brought you lunch too. I can't stay long. I left Natalie at the store, and I have to get back."

Helen answered. "That's okay, dear. I was just about to make lunch for Cole as my way of thanking him for his help."

She urged me to play along by giving me a look.

"Cole, surely you have time to stay for a little lunch before you head back?"

Before I could answer good, Will yelled from the living room, "I thought he was here to talk about..."

Helen didn't let him finish. She spoke right over him.

"Will, it's time to eat your lunch so you can take your medicine, dear."

This was pure comedy at this point. It felt like the best-laid plans were slowly starting to unravel. If we could manage to pull this off without Payton figuring out why I was really there, it would be a miracle.

"Okay, well, I brought all of your favorites. There are a couple of chicken salad sandwiches with a side of fruit and an assortment of cookies."

I loved the way Payton took care of everyone. There were a lot of qualities about her that reminded me of my late wife, Laura. Of course, Payton had her own unique way that drew me in and allowed me to fall in love.

"A woman who knows how to spoil her family. I like it," I said.

"This was a nice surprise. Seeing you made my day."

We embraced briefly as she prepared to head back to work. I wanted to kiss her and hold her for a little while but thought it would be best to save it for when we were alone.

"Mom, Dad, Cole...love you. Enjoy your lunch." She blew a kiss goodbye and headed out the door.

"Love you too. Thanks for lunch, sweetheart," Will responded.

As soon as Payton was out the door, I breathed a sigh of relief.

"Wow, that was a close call!" Helen said.

"Yes, but you handled it like a pro. I was desperately trying to come up with something, and you saved the day with the sink excuse."

"I've had my fair share of having to keep secrets in this family. With all the birthdays, holidays, surprise parties, you name it. If you don't know how to keep a secret with three kids, you'll quickly find yourself up the creek without a paddle."

"I'll bet. Well, before we go any further, I feel like I have to get this out before anything else crazy happens today."

Will joined us in the kitchen to prepare for lunch.

"As I started to mention on the phone, Payton is very special to me. I never thought in a million years that I would ever meet someone who would captivate my heart and win over my daughter's heart the way Payton has."

They stood still and listened intently to what I had to say.

"I find it to be rather amazing that the three of us began forming our own bond well before I knew Payton existed. From the beginning, I've always regarded the two of you as more than just clients, and I hope you feel the same way about me."

"You know we do." Helen placed her hands over her mouth in anticipation of what I was about to say.

"I'm glad. With that in mind, I think Payton and I have what it takes to build a good life together. I love her. When I look at her, I see the woman of my dreams and a wonderful step-mother to my child. I see my lover and my best friend. With that being said, I came here to ask for your blessing as I prepare to ask for her hand in marriage."

I'm not sure I could make out what Helen was saying. She was all choked up with emotion. Her arms flew open, and she welcomed me to the family with tears in her eyes. She sobbed tears of joy for what seemed like an eternity.

"Will, aren't you so happy? Come here, honey. Our Payton is getting married. And this time, he's a good catch!"

"It's about time our youngest finally got married." Will had his daughters mixed up.

"Honey, I'm talking about Payton, not Rebecca. Cole is going to ask Payton to marry him."

"Right. Isn't that nice? I'm so happy for you, Cole."

"Thank you, Sir." We gave each other a firm hug.

"I feel so relieved now that I have your blessing."

"Cole, did you ever doubt that you would have our blessing?" Helen said.

"No, but a man can never be too certain. I just wanted to make sure I went about this the right way."

"We appreciate the thought and consideration, but you have to know that I've been your biggest fan from day one. The first time I saw the two of you together at the Inn, I remember thinking you would make a good match. Will tried to get me to stay out of it, but that's just not in my DNA."

Will sniggled as he sat down and took the first bite out of his sandwich.

"Please eat, Cole. Clearly, William is helping himself already. There's no need for us to stand here and starve. I know you have to get back to work soon, but I'd hate for you to leave here hungry."

"Thanks, Helen."

I took a seat at the table with them and thought this was the perfect time to ask for some marital advice.

"If you don't mind me asking, what are the key ingredients that have helped you and Will to sustain a long and happy marriage?"

"Hmm," she said while eating her fruit.

"It would have to be the fact that we were already best friends, strong communication, and knowing when to agree to disagree."

"Well said. Thankfully, I think we have the key ingredients you described. That, coupled with our love for Emmie, makes me feel pretty blessed."

"As you should. You all will make a beautiful family together. Do you already have an idea of what you want to do for the proposal?" she asked.

"I'm glad you mentioned it. I still have a few details that need to be ironed out, but I was hoping to elicit your help."

"Oooh, this is so exciting. What can I do?"

"Well, since the Fourth of July is coming up soon, I thought we could make this a family affair at my place. We can grill, enjoy the sunset, and the fireworks on the beach. This way, Payton will think we're just gathering and will have no idea about what's to come. What do you think?"

She jumped up and squeezed me. To me, it only made sense that those who were close to us would be involved. We're all very big on family.

She took her seat again.

"Everyone is going to love being a part of this," Helen said.

"Perfect. If you can just make arrangements for Abby, Wyatt, the kids, and Rebecca to be at my house around two, that would be perfect. Rebecca can even bring a plus one if she'd like. I'll make sure there's plenty of food, and I'll tell Payton that we want to have you guys over for a cookout. How does that sound?"

"It's perfect. She won't suspect a thing."

"I knew you were the person to help pull this off, Helen."

"You bet. But aren't you under pressure time-wise? The fourth is just a couple of weeks away."

"I think I can do it. "

Will excused himself from the table. As he passed me by, he stopped and rested his hand on my shoulder.

"Good luck to you, son. You'll have to excuse me while I head back to my recliner."

Will was sticking to his routine just as Helen had promised. I was just so happy to know that he seemed please with the proposal. I knew this would mean the world to Payton.

"Thank you, Will."

I turned to Helen. "I guess this would be a good time for me to head back to work. I have a basement renovation waiting for my finishing touch."

"I'm sure it's going to be a beauty," she said.

I was so thankful for my future in-laws. I confirmed a date for us to check-in regarding plans for the fourth. Afterward, I left feeling really good about things. The next task before me... planning the most romantic proposal that Payton has ever experienced and will never forget.

PAYTON

*I*t was the morning of the fourth of July. I laid in bed, contemplating if I had made the right decision to close the store for the day. I don't know why I worried about it so much. My sales were doing well, and most families wouldn't be concerned about taking pictures today. My quiet thought time was interrupted by a knock on my bedroom door.

"Payton, it's me. Are you awake?" I thought it was funny that mom always asks me if I'm awake. If I wasn't, I guess that would be my cue to get up anyway.

"Come on in. Just lying here being lazy," I said.

She entered sounding more energetic than usual and plopped down at the foot of the bed.

"Happy Fourth of July!"

"Somebody is bright-eyed and chipper this morning. Happy fourth to you too!"

"Well, there's a lot to be excited about. For one, you're actually home on a Saturday morning. That's unheard of."

"Funny you should mention it. I was just laying here questioning my decision to close for the day."

"I don't know why. Both you and Natalie deserve a day off. I could understand if you had a clothing store but come on, Payton. You need to take a long and hard look at your holidays for the remainder of the year as well."

"I will, Mom. So what's on your mind this morning? I know you didn't come in here just to wish me a happy fourth."

"No, I didn't. I was in the kitchen, getting the ingredients together for my strawberry shortcake. I thought it might be nice to make some to bring to Cole's this afternoon. What do you think?"

"Are you talking about the one where you make the whipped cream and biscuits from scratch?"

"That's the one!" she said.

"My mouth is watering just thinking about it. Let me know if you need help. I could use a few pointers for making summer desserts."

"Wonderful. But first we have to start with breakfast. How about I whip up some scrambled eggs and bacon? Maybe even pancakes if you'd like?"

"Mom, you sure know how to spoil me. What will I ever do when I finally move out of here and find my own place?"

"You'll take all of my recipes with you and carry on the tradition plus add to it and create some of your own," she said.

"True."

"You and dad don't know how grateful I am for the extra time I've had here with you. It really helped me while getting the business on its feet. I wouldn't have saved a penny if I did it any other way."

"I remember those days. We were practically broke for the first couple of years after opening the Inn. Somehow we managed to hang in there."

"Do you miss the Inn?" I asked Mom.

"I do. Our livelihood existed at the Inn. I miss the friendships and day to day things that would keep us on our toes. Now it seems like we've very quickly fallen into a routine at home. I'm thankful, but it doesn't look anything like our original retirement plans," mom said.

"Maybe that's something I can help you work on. I know it frightened you the day dad got lost, but he made it home safe. You can't let that scare you into staying home all the time."

"I guess you're right."

"You know what we should do for fun?" I said.

"What?"

"We should go visit the Inn and see what they've done with the place. I bet it will bring back nice memories."

"Either that or all the changes they've made will make me cry."

"Oh, come on, Mom. This isn't like you at all. At least give it a try."

"I will. In the meantime, we have a fun afternoon to prepare for. Time to get up and get on the good foot!"

She marched out of the room chanting, "Left, left, left, right, left. I'll see you in the kitchen in ten minutes."

When the door closed, I buried myself back under the covers. The Lord knows he didn't gift me with the ability to be an early morning person.

Later that afternoon, I drove mom and dad over to Cole's house. I was impressed with how well he decorated the beach house to give it a patriotic feel. I thought surely he had help from Alice and Emmie because the place looked spectacular.

When we arrived, we walked around back to find everyone mingling and talking.

"Here they are." Alice was the first to greet us with Emmie following closely behind.

"Hi, Alice. Happy Fourth of July," I said.

"Same to you, Payton. Don't you look pretty."

"Thank you. It's going to be a challenge to keep this all-white sundress free from barbecue sauce."

"Oh, I'm sure you'll manage just fine."

She went on to say hello to my parents and find a cool spot for my dad to sit.

"Emmie, look at you all color-coordinated red, white, and blue from head to toe."

She wore the cutest bathing suit top with color-coordinated shorts. All of the kids were in their swimwear and looked like they were ready to hit the beach.

"My tongue is color coordinated too. See." She stuck out her tongue to show me the evidence of red and blue popsicles. My niece and nephew did the same.

"I used to love eating the Firecracker popsicles when I was a little girl. I hope you saved one for me."

"We did. There's extra in the freezer."

Cole came over and welcomed me with a kiss and brushed my hair into place with his fingers. I always loved it when he showed affection.

"Eww, gross," the kids said in total disgust.

"Hey, you say that now, but I bet you'll change your tune when you're my age," Cole said.

We kissed one more time before sneaking a peek at my mother's strawberry shortcake.

"Mmm, what do we have here?"

Mom was quick to answer as she secured the dish, "It's my signature strawberry shortcake. I made plenty for everyone to enjoy after dinner."

"She doesn't play around with her desserts, Cole. She usually has to keep a close watch, so dessert doesn't disappear before dinner is served," Rebecca warned.

"That's because we have two dessert thieves in our midst," Abby said.

"Who...me?" I pointed to myself, pretending not to know what she was talking about.

"Yes, you and Rebecca. It never fails. Mom puts the dessert out on the table for everyone to enjoy, and these two go back for seconds and thirds. Before you know it, it's all gone, and they're standing around blaming each other."

"I plead the fifth," Rebecca said.

"Okay, Miss Lawyer A.K.A dessert thief," I said.

Just as we were teasing each other and having fun, I heard a knocking sound on the deck.

"Hello, everybody!" Ethan said.

My mouth opened at the site of Ethan, walking over to give Rebecca a hug. I hadn't seen him in ages. He looked good in his docker shorts and beach sandals. She was always a sucker for the preppy type, and Ethan definitely fit the bill.

"That's her old high school sweetheart," I whispered to Cole.

Cole didn't really know the history behind Ethan and Rebecca. I'd have to fill him in on the whole story later on.

Ethan walked around and said hello to all of the family. Dad couldn't remember him but played along as best as he could. My mother just about cried. In her heart of hearts, Ethan was supposed to become a future son in law after their college graduation.

"Payton, I understand congratulations are in order." He headed towards me with his arms wide open. Before I could clarify what he was talking about, Rebecca started clearing her throat so loud I almost forgot my trend of thought.

"Are you alright?" I asked her.

"Oh, I'm fine. Something must've gone down the wrong pipe." She gave Ethan a funny look.

I refocused my attention on Ethan. "I'm sorry. What were you saying?"

"Ethan was congratulating you on opening up your new store. I told him all about it," Rebecca answered.

"Ohhhh, the store. Yes, of course. Thank you. How have you been, Ethan?"

"I've been well. My time in California was pretty nice, but as they say, there's no place like home."

"Well, I'm so glad you're back. It's really good to see you. Allow me to introduce you to Cole."

Cole shook Ethan's hand.

"Cole, nice to meet you. Thanks for extending an invitation."

"Likewise, I'm glad to have you."

Alice tapped her glass with a fork to get everyone's attention.

"Welcome, everyone. Although this is officially my son's gathering, he called upon me to help in the catering department."

Everyone laughed. I think by now, it was common knowledge that Cole couldn't cook.

"I did elicit a little help from him. And by help, I mean that he turned on the grill and set up the ice bucket."

Wyatt shouted, "Come on, man, you can do better than that. At least put the meat on the grill."

Again there was more laughter.

"You tell him, Wyatt." Mom teased.

"But seriously, there's corn on the cob, potato salad, and plenty of food from the grill for everyone. And don't forget to leave room for Helen's strawberry shortcake when you're done. Please dig in and enjoy!"

It felt so good to spend the day with the family. We all ate and laughed and then ate and laughed some more. We took the kids down to the shore and let them play until their hearts were content. I even took a few photos to capture the occasion and add to my family album.

Around sunset, Cole came to the kitchen to make an announcement.

"Alright, everyone. Every year it's a tradition that Emmie and I have a front-row seat on the beach to see the spectacular fireworks. This year we've planned something extra special that you don't want to miss."

"Payton, if you will join me, I have a front-row seat planned especially for you."

I took his hand and followed his lead. The family followed behind us. On the beach, we entered a path of tiki torches that were beautifully lit.

"Cole, this is so pretty."

"I'm glad you like it. There's more at the end of the path," he said.

I looked behind me to see everyone following a few feet behind. Several of them had cameras in hand recording Cole and me. He started to speak.

"It wasn't long ago that I walked into the Inn at Pelican Beach. I can close my eyes and see you standing at the front desk just like it was yesterday. You were so beautiful then, and you're even more beautiful to me now."

He stopped at the end of the path where there was a bed of red roses in the shape of a heart.

I could feel the tears immediately start running down my face. He took me by the hand and helped me step inside the heart with him.

"As time progressed, we grew in friendship, you welcomed Emmie into your heart, and then we fell in love. I didn't think I could fall in love again. You showed me that I was wrong. I created this heart that we're standing in as a symbol to demonstrate that you will forever have a place inside my heart. With that being said, there's one more symbol that I want to show you."

Cole put his arm around me and pointed up to the sky as the fireworks began. An array of colors started falling from the sky. Then just as big as ever the words formed in bold red letters 'Payton Will You Marry Me?' As the colors continued to burst forth, Cole got down on one knee.

"Payton, will you give me the honor of becoming my wife?" He presented me with a sparkling diamond ring.

I felt a big lump in my throat that made it difficult to speak. Somehow I still managed to belt out the word yes loud enough for everyone to hear.

"Yes! Oh my gosh, yes!"

He placed the ring on my finger and planted a kiss that gave me butterflies. We held each other for what seemed like forever while the fireworks continued to light up the sky.

The family cheered and whistled like a bunch of hooligans in the background. Cole signaled for them to join us.

"She said yes!!"

The cameras flashed, and the videos continued to record.

"She said yes!!" He repeated.

I hugged mom and dad and continued right on down the line exchanging tears along with hugs and kisses.

"I can't believe y'all knew about this and didn't say a word."

"Mr. Ethan almost blew the secret," Emmie said.

"He sure did, but we cleaned it up just in time." Rebecca agreed.

I don't know how I managed to go through the whole day without suspecting anything, but Cole pulled it off. There was no way I would be able to sleep tonight, but I didn't care. Tonight was absolutely the best night of my life.

EPILOGUE: PAYTON

*J*anuary 1st had come and gone so quickly I hardly could believe it. Cole and I decided on a July wedding, but with six months left, we still hadn't made up our minds about a venue. Today I was meeting Rebecca and Abby for lunch so they could help me wrap my head around a few wedding plans.

"I need your help. I thought surely I'd be done with all the wedding planning by now, and the rest of the planning would be a cakewalk. Instead, I'm really starting to stress out."

"What on earth do you have to stress out about? You are marrying the most easy-going guy in the world. Cole doesn't care where you guys get married. And it's not like this is your first rodeo. You've done this before. You got this," Abby said.

"Then why is it starting to feel so complicated? We can't seem to settle on a venue to save our lives. We visited at least eight places and even considered traveling as far as Naples. No matter where we visited, there was either something wrong with the dates, the venue itself, or the food."

Abby and I dug right into our food when it was served. I

noticed Rebecca hadn't touched hers and seemed rather distant.

"Well, maybe it's time for you guys to brainstorm and start thinking out of the box. For example, does it have to be a traditional venue type of wedding?" Abby said.

"If not at a venue, then where? Hold that thought for a minute. Rebecca, are you okay? You don't seem like yourself at all."

"I'm fine. I'm probably just exhausted from work. That plus flying back and forth to Savannah twice a month is probably starting to catch up with me."

"I'm not going to say I told you so. However, I knew taking on that house was biting off more than you could chew," I said.

"So basically you're not going to say 'I told you so'... you're just going to find another way to say 'I told you so.' Rebecca snapped back at me, so I decided to back down.

"Look, all I'm trying to say is that's a big undertaking. Have you considered hiring some extra help?"

"That's a good idea," Abby said.

"Believe it or not, the renovations are coming along very nicely. I'm forever grateful for Cole making a few calls and suggesting the company that I'm working with. The contractors are doing a phenomenal job, they've tried to help me cut cost without taking away from the quality, and overall I'm really pleased."

"That's wonderful." I kept listening as I ate.

"Sooo, how are things with Ethan?" Abby and I both wanted the scoop. As of late, Rebecca had become increasingly tight-lipped about their relationship.

"Things are good. I don't want to blow it out of proportion and make it sound like more than what it is, but so far, so good."

"Come on, Rebecca. Spill the darn tea already. Whenever

we're together, you barely talk about Ethan. We've seen him maybe two or three times in the past six months," Abby said.

"Yeah, and I know for a fact that whenever I stop by your place, you're never home. What's up with that?"

We sat and waited for a response.

"If you must know, everything is good, just as I told you. We've been dating exclusively for a couple of months now, but I didn't want to make a big deal about it, that's all," she said.

I couldn't believe she'd been holding back.

"Um, hello! You didn't think that was worth mentioning? Do you know how happy mom would be to hear that her dream has finally coming to fruition?"

"That's exactly why I didn't want to say anything. I don't want mom to get all excited and start trying to walk me down the aisle before I'm ready. I can just hear her now. I don't have any guarantees of a future with Ethan like you do with Cole."

Again she snapped at me, but I tried to remain patient.

"I get it if you want to take your time with Ethan. But keeping it all to yourself and not bringing him around the family just seems silly if you ask me."

"Payton always has the answers to everything, doesn't she?" Rebecca murmured.

"What has gotten into you?" I could tell Abby's switch had been flipped.

"Nothing. I'm sorry. It's me. I probably should've passed on lunch today. I'm just not feeling like myself," Rebecca said.

She put on her jacket and left a hundred dollar bill on the table.

"Here, lunch is on me. Maybe we can reschedule for another day. Payton, I'd really like to help you with wedding planning. I pulled a few ideas for you to look through in this folder."

Rebecca passed me the folder and proceeded to get up.

"I'm going to head home. I'll give you guys a call later on."

She pushed her chair in and made it about six feet away from the table before passing out on the floor.

"Rebecca!" I yelled.

We ran to her aid and stayed by her side while the staff cleared the area. Abby dialed 911. By the time the paramedics arrived and placed her on a gurney, she had regained total consciousness.

"What happened?" She tried to talk.

"You fell out in the middle of the restaurant and nearly scared me to death," I said.

She looked horrified. "I wonder what that was about?"

"Girl, you can't scare us like that." Abby held Rebecca's hand.

"I promise I wasn't trying to," she said.

"I know. Listen, Payton will ride with you in the ambulance, and I'll follow behind you in the car. Everything will be alright."

"Thanks, Abby," Rebecca said.

We were at the hospital for hours. When my parents and Ethan arrived, Abby went home to be with the kids. I stuck around to hear the results from Rebecca's blood work.

"Ms. Matthews, can I come in?" The doctor knocked on the door.

"Sure, come on in, Doc. I hope you don't mind the extra company." She introduced us briefly and then waited to hear what the doctor had to say.

"Well, I stopped by to give you good news."

"Oh, that's a sigh of relief. I can handle good news." Rebecca's demeanor immediately shifted to a more relaxed state.

"Yes, congratulations are in order to you and the family," the doctor said.

"What do you mean?" Rebecca propped herself up, looking clueless as the doctor spoke.

"According to my calendar, you're about eight weeks pregnant."

It's a wonder Rebecca didn't pass out in the bed right where she was lying.

"You have got to be kidding me," she said.

"I don't kid about these things, Ms. Matthews." She continued to sit there, looking stunned by the news.

Everyone's reaction was priceless. Mom sat with her mouth wide open. So much till I thought her odds for catching a fly were extremely high. Dad kept repeatedly asking mom, "You alright, dear?." And then there was Ethan who finally broke his silence and started crying and hugging Rebecca.

"I'm going to be a father!"

"Unbelievable... Un... believable," Rebecca said. She was still in phase one of total shock.

"How did this happen?" Mom finally spoke out, but we all just looked at her. This was no time to get into life lessons about the birds and the bees.

Later that evening, we saw to it that Rebecca had everything she needed at home to be comfortable. Mom and I agreed to give Rebecca and Ethan some time together but not before mom shared a few parting words.

"My youngest is having a baby." She hugged Rebecca and nestled her close as only a mom could.

"If I know right, you're probably afraid, aren't you?"

"Yes. I knew that I haven't been feeling good, but I thought maybe it was the flu or a stomach bug of some sort. I don't know if I'm fit to be a mother," she said.

I sat on the other side of the bed and listened as mom provided words of comfort to Rebecca.

"I felt the same exact way when I was pregnant with Abby.

It was my first time, and I had no idea what I was doing. And do you know what my mother told me?"

"What?"

"She said, 'As long as you love her and take care of her needs, what could possibly go wrong?' And when I truly stopped to think about it, she was right. So I did just as mom advised. When Abby was born, your father and I took care of her needs and loved her unconditionally. Did we make mistakes along the way? Absolutely. We did with all of our children. But in the end, you all turned out just fine."

"All of us? I don't know, Mom. Rebecca is kind of special." I teased.

"Be quiet, Payton." She cracked a smile while wiping away her tears.

"Here's what I want to know. You know how much I adore Ethan. I've always wanted the two of you to become an item. Why wasn't I aware the two of you were together?"

Rebecca looked over at me, but I pretended to be looking up at the ceiling.

"There was no real reason other than I wanted to make sure this time was for real. I figured if I started bringing him to our weekly family dinners and to every event, then you all would assume we were on a serious path again. I needed to confirm what path we were on for myself first. "Imagine the embarrassment of being let down by the same guy twice?"

"Ohh, Rebecca. Honey, you have to let the past go. The past is exactly where it belongs. In the past! Did you see how excited that man was to learn he's about to be a father?"

"Yeah, after he stood frozen in a two-minute coma," she said.

"I think you need to show him a little grace. We all were in a two-minute coma!"

"That's true," Rebecca said.

"Ethan has loved you since the moment he laid eyes on you. Even if that was back in high school, he certainly didn't take long to recapture your heart once he returned to Pelican Beach. If you ask me, there's a reason why the other guys you dated never worked out. The one who you were truly meant to be with had already been chosen for you a long time ago."

In true girl fashion, we huddled at Rebecca's bedside and cried, hugged, and laughed together. Our lives were proof that things didn't always go according to plan. However, some of the best-laid plans were made to be broken and even turned out better that way.

A Pelican Beach Affair - Pelican Beach Series Book 3

Ready to read Book 3 in the Pelican Beach series?

In this third installment of the Pelican Beach series, Payton and Cole are back, and they're ready to commence their union. It sounds easy enough, but will life circumstances keep them apart?

The theme of new beginnings continues as Rebecca and Ethan prepare to welcome their firstborn. However, these two have a lot more to figure out besides navigating parenthood. With the clock winding down before the baby's arrival, will they decide to make things official by getting married?

Lastly, we can't forget about Cole's mother, Alice. She spent many years looking after the family. She's been the perfect grandmother, and supportive when Cole needed her most. But it's been a long time since she's had someone to call her own. Will she continue her life's journey as a single woman? Or perhaps find herself in the middle of a love triangle?

The Matthews are back, and they're sure to take you on a journey. You might find yourself crying, laughing, or ready to give a character a piece of your mind. Either way, pull up a beach chair and get ready to be entangled in A Pelican Beach Affair.

Also By Michele Gilcrest

Pelican Beach Series

The Inn At Pelican Beach: Book 1

Sunsets At Pelican Beach: Book 2

A Pelican Beach Affair: Book 3

Christmas At Pelican Beach: Book 4

Cortland Series

Second Time Around: Book 1

Tried and True : Book 2

CPSIA information can be obtained
at www.ICGtesting.com
Printed in the USA
BVHW080233030321
601495BV00011B/1172